I0642730

TASTE OF DEATH

Ravenous Spirits Series
BOOK 1

RON RIPLEY

EDITED BY ANNE LAO
AND DAWN KLEMISH

ISBN: 979-8-89476-315-6
Copyright © 2025 by ScareStreet.com

All rights reserved. This book or any portion thereof may not be reproduced or used in any manner whatsoever without written permission from the publisher except for the use of brief quotations in a book review.

This is a work of fiction. Any resemblance to actual persons, living or dead, or actual events is purely coincidental.

Enter the Realm of Terror…

We'd like to take a moment to thank you for your support and invite you to join our VIP newsletter.

Dive deeper into the darkness with exclusive offers, early access to new releases, and bone-chilling deals when you sign up at www.ScareStreet.com.

Let the nightmares begin…

See you in the shadows,
Scare Street

PROLOGUE

The air was crisp enough to sting the lungs. It would be another hour before the sun rose, and even then, the gray skies would not allow lights to penetrate. It had been a long time since the sun's warmth had touched the island.

Jackson had been on the island for just four months. He should have waited until warmer weather. He should have trusted his gut and waited for spring, but he had been so excited about the idea of joining an intentional community. A hippie commune, his dad would have called it. Never mind that no one had been a hippie in more than half a century. None of that mattered, though.

Maple Grove had seemed like a dream when Jackson's friend, Alina, told him about it. The tiny island community near the Canadian border sustained itself with an artisanal maple harvest, fishing, farming, and community effort. People working together to support one another. Hard work, kindness, and understanding. A community the way it was supposed to be, where people gave a damn.

Growing up in the city, Jackson had always felt detached from the world. There were neighbors his family didn't know, who didn't want to be known. People were rushed, brusque, disinterested, and selfish. Everything was in pursuit of more money, more power, and more stuff. So many people got stepped on so that one person could reach the top. He hated to think that was the way the world was meant to be. In fact, he refused to believe it.

He'd met Alina in college, and she was a bright light in the darkness. She was studying biology with the intent to become a large animal veterinarian. She loved life, she loved nature, and she was so kind. No one was beneath her. Everyone was worthy of her time and respect. She was the most beautiful person he had met.

The relationship had never blossomed into what Jackson wanted it to be. He was in love with her, and that was obvious to most people. He even told her once. She told him she loved him too but as a friend. Alina loved everyone. He couldn't fault her for it. In the end, he ended up loving her more.

They had shared a dream of a place they could live that wasn't bound by the unspoken rules of society. A place that didn't prioritize greed and wealth and selfishness. He had never asked her how she discovered Maple Grove. She knew all kinds of like-minded people who were into similar things. He assumed she'd learned about it from someone who'd learned about it from someone.

She had lived on the island for a month when she got in touch with him and told him about it. After they graduated college, he wasn't sure he would get to spend any serious time with her again. She was constantly on the go. He leaped at the opportunity to be with her again, especially in a place that sounded so wonderful.

The first week on the island was a thrill. The people were welcoming, the landscape was beautiful, and Alina was there with him every day. She showed him around, helped him set up a place to live in one of the tiny houses that was already there, and made sure everyone met him while singing his praises.

On his first night in Maple Grove, she stayed up with him all night while they shared stories, ate junk food, and just laughed and enjoyed each other's company. She was beautiful beyond words, and he wanted nothing more than to lean across the slightly threadbare little sofa he had been provided and kiss her. He felt like he had found heaven on earth. But that didn't last.

Snow crunched under Jackson's feet. The path from the town to the dock was normally not so exhausting, but traveling in darkness through the densely packed snow considerably slowed his progress. Each footstep was a struggle to pull out of the hole he'd dug for himself. He wanted to go faster. He needed to go faster. It was just not feasible.

The island was not what he thought it was. It was not what Alina thought it was. He warned her about what he had seen, but she didn't believe him. She thought he was using again. They had done their fair share of drugs in college, but he had been clean for more than a year.

Even when he told her point-blank that the people on the island were dangerous, and that he had seen something come out of the woods, she rationalized it to him. She told him that some of the Elders had probably slipped him something with mushrooms in it. They were reckless like that sometimes. They liked to haze the newcomers a little.

The things they believed, though, and the mythology they had come up with on the island just got into his head. It made him see things that weren't there.

She told him that it was all just stories. There was nothing to be afraid of on the island. All their talk of nature spirits, death and rebirth—all of that was just metaphor. They were people who held the earth in high esteem. So what if they created stories about spirits of the woods helping grow the harvest? It was just something to unite the community. He had to stop taking it literally and be rational. That's what she said.

He wanted to believe her. He wanted nothing more than to live in that place with her and maybe show her that he could be more than a friend. Maybe one day, she could love him the way that he loved her. But he knew in his heart he hadn't taken anything. He wasn't seeing things, and she would never believe him. Why would she? The things he was saying were crazy.

Jackson had seen a monster. A demon. Maybe the devil; he didn't know. It was a nightmare come to life, and he wouldn't stay there any longer. He needed to get help. He needed to find someone to save the people on the island before it was too late. The people who couldn't or wouldn't believe what was happening. People like Alina.

He thought leaving would be easy. He would just tell them he wanted to go back to the mainland for a day, no big deal. But the Elders had immediately shut the idea down. If anyone wanted to leave, they needed to book passage on a boat a week in advance.

He had done that, but they had told him it wasn't a good time. The weather was bad one day, and another day, the boat needed to be repaired. There was more than one boat on the island, but there was always a problem.

Jackson wanted to at least call his father, but that became an issue, too. He had not brought a phone to the island with him. Alina told him they didn't use technology like that, but there was a phone for emergencies. Except the phone was down every time he asked. The radios on the boats were down as well. They didn't even try to come up with good excuses.

Jackson thought his last letter to his father had gotten out on the mail boat, but he couldn't be sure. He had never had reason to doubt any of it during the first few weeks of his stay, but now, he wondered how many of his letters went out. His father had written back twice, while Jackson had sent more than ten letters. He wasn't writing to converse, just updating his dad on what was going on so he knew not to worry.

Most of the letters Jackson sent were mundane, just letting his dad know about the island and how much he enjoyed it. He had sent one expressing his concerns just after the first time he'd asked to leave. Since then, he had seen more things in the dark. He had seen what was in the woods, and he was desperate to get off the island. He couldn't understand why they didn't want to go at first, but it slowly dawned on him.

The Elders on the island didn't disbelieve him. They knew what he was talking about, they just didn't want him to tell anyone. To Jackson, that meant they had to keep him quiet. What he had seen was real, and his life was in danger.

There were no roads on the island. There were footpaths, and if there had been no snow, he could have followed them. Everything on the island was done the hard way. The old way. Goods were carried by hand. Wheelbarrows and carts could be moved under manpower, but there weren't even horses for labor. Everything was earned by the sweat of someone's brow. It made things hard. It made getting to the dock hard.

Jackson heard the ocean in the distance. He heard the water as it reached the edge of the island, lapping at the stone, and promising a way out. But it was still so dark. He could see almost nothing.

Another sound reached his ears. The crunching of snow underfoot. He was far enough from the village that the people wouldn't hear him. No one should have known that he'd even left. There'd be no reason for someone to check on him until morning. But he could have sworn he heard footsteps behind him.

He stopped and stood still in the cold, holding his breath. One step. Just one, but it came after he stopped moving. Someone was following him.

Jackson turned and looked back across the snow-covered field. No one was there. The village lay in the distance past hills and small maple groves. Between him and it were only snowbanks and random, single trees. Barely room for anyone to hide.

He stared at the nearest of the trees, straining his eyes in the darkness. It could have hidden someone. Something. If they were fast, they could have ducked behind it.

Jackson fought the urge to call out and ask who was there. There could be no reply that would satisfy him. Anyone not wishing him harm would not have hidden. And calling out might draw undue attention from others. He wanted neither.

With a long exhale of misty breath, Jackson turned and began to run. It was clumsy and slow. The snow forbade it from being productive, but his pursuer would be just as unsuccessful at chasing him down.

He needed to get to a boat. He planned to steal one. The police could bring it back later if it came to that. He could pilot any of the boats the islanders used easily enough. He just needed to get away.

His breathing became heavy and labored faster than he had expected. It was so much effort to run through the snow, but he made progress. He was getting closer to the path that led down the hillside to the docks that waited below.

The crunching of his boots in the snow was almost deafening. He thought he heard a second set in pursuit, but it was hard to tell, and he didn't want to stop to check this time. If he stopped, his pursuer could catch him. He couldn't risk it.

He saw the path ahead of him now, murky in the ambient light of night where it led down the island's hillside to the docks. He was close if he could manage the potentially treacherous path in the snow. The way was not too steep, but it was winding and potentially obscured.

At the edge of the snow-covered path atop the hill, Jackson turned to look back the way he had come. The sound of pursuing footsteps was so clear now. Someone was trudging through the snow after him at speed. But when he looked, there was no one.

"What the...?"

The word was barely a whisper as he stared in confusion. He had heard it so distinctly. He knew someone was there. But now there was nothing.

Jackson turned, not willing to waste another moment worrying about it. Two boats were on the dock. He could just make them out in the dark. Either one would suffice. Then he could be free and, hopefully, find a way to convince Alina to leave the island as well. Once he came back with help.

He turned back toward the sea and took his first step onto the hidden, snow-encrusted path to the water. Something snagged at his foot, jerking at his ankle, and pulling him back hard enough to throw him off-balance. Jackson barely cried out before he tumbled forward, face-first into the snow.

Gravity took over, and Jackson rolled down the hill. Blasts of pain erupted across his body as he hit unseen obstacles under the snow. Rocks, roots, barren shrubs, and other unseen dangers scratched at his clothing and prodded at his flesh.

The world spun in a frenzy of freezing cold and sharp pain until finally, his head smashed against something hard, and he could no longer tell if it was him spinning or everything around him. It didn't matter anymore. As quickly as it happened, everything faded to black.

✳ ✳ ✳

The sound of footsteps. Was someone still after him? That sound of harsh, crunching snow. But there was more. Jackson felt it. Fingers of freezing cold running across his back and sliding up under his jacket.

He opened his eyes. His head hurt, and there was a throbbing pain just above his left temple. He was moving, face-up, and looking at the blank, dark sky. Snow scraped up his back as someone dragged him through the forest.

"Stop." Jackson struggled weakly. "Stop!"

Something colder than the ice on his back gripped his ankle. It felt like steel threatening to crush bone. He thought at first that he was dragged by a chain, but when he lifted his head to see what it was, he saw a man.

Upside down, woozy, and in the dark, Jackson found it hard to focus. He blinked to make out details of who was dragging him and where they were taking him. The man pulling him was not wearing clothes despite the deadly temperature.

It took only a moment for Jackson to realize what was wrong. It was not a man dragging him. It was what he had seen in the woods. Torn flesh and open wounds. Bones and rot and death.

Jackson struggled to pull free. The thing pulling him didn't slow, didn't even bother to look back at him. It just continued trudging through the darkness.

"Let me go!" Jackson kicked out with his other foot. His attacks missed their mark as if the thing pulling him wasn't there. He could not hit it. He could not get away.

He yelled for help and reached out for stumps of weeds and shrubs to hold on and pull himself free. The thing pulling him never slowed or lost its grip. Even when Jackson thought he had a hold of something to anchor himself, the power of his assailant was more than he could overcome, and his hands pulled free.

They stopped suddenly, and Jackson, shivering from the cold and breathing heavily, sat up. The thing had dragged him deep into the woods and into a clearing he did not recognize. It was gone when he lifted his head.

"What…?"

The question never fully left his lips. The thought barely even formed before a searing pain unlike any he had experienced cut into his arm.

Jackson tried to pull away but could not. His head swam as he saw it. *Really* saw it. Flesh was peeled down to the bone across its forehead. A single eye was lodged in the exposed skull and caked with old, rotten meat.

Teeth were buried in Jackson's flesh. The rotten thing chewed off a piece, and he watched as its jaws worked. Blood gushed from the wound, from an exposed artery that had been torn. Jackson tried to pull away, to twist his body and gain any kind of leverage to free himself, but could not.

The thing bit him again, pulling away a mouthful of meat. Jackson screamed. He continued screaming for as long as he could, with each new bite and mouthful, until the cold and weakness overwhelmed him. Soon, he barely felt what was happening. But the thing kept eating.

The last thing Jackson heard was the sound of his bones snapping, but he couldn't feel it.

CHAPTER 1
A FAVOR

A crow sat on the fence post. It had been ages since Shane remembered seeing a bird on the property.

He watched it from the kitchen window as he drank from his cup of coffee. No one had spoken in minutes; he wasn't sure how long. The scene would have looked absurd to anyone who stumbled upon it. Shane and a handful of ghosts—Eloise, the triplets, Carl, and Herbert—staring at a bird as if they were at a zoo and getting their money's worth.

The ghosts were enamored with the scene. Eloise had developed an affinity for the local wildlife. She had unofficially adopted a small gang of cats out in the neighborhood. Carl was more of a surprise to Shane. Carl did not seem like birds would be his thing, at least not for such a long time. But the silence was nice, so Shane didn't interrupt it.

"In the carnival, most animals didn't want to be around our tents," Herbert said

"Animals usually shun the dead," Carl agreed.

"Not all of them. Cats like me," Eloise pointed out.

"I had a cat once," Daphne added.

They fell back into silence, watching the bird as it sat almost perfectly still doing nothing. Shane finished his coffee and pondered a second cup as he fished around in his pocket for a pack of cigarettes.

"Crows are omens," Herbert said. "That's what my mother used to say. Bad omens."

"Death omens," Carl said.

"We're all already dead," Daisy said.

Eloise glanced over her shoulder at Shane, who shrugged and lifted his lighter, setting flame to the tip of the cigarette. He had no doubt death would come for him someday, but he doubted that it sent birds to let him know ahead of time.

When the knock came at the door, no one was expecting it. Everyone had been distracted by the bird outside, so it was more of a surprise than usual. Shane almost laughed at the tension when something caught the ghosts off-guard.

He left the room first, letting them worry about what it meant that they could all be so easily rattled. Shane was not expecting any visitors, and his neighbors never stopped by to say hello. From the outside, the house was enough to persuade anyone who had no business there to stay away.

Shane opened the door and was met with a familiar face. Frank Benedict stood on his porch, a hat covering his bald head for a change of pace, and a thick-looking winter jacket to keep him warm in the inclement weather. Winter was approaching, and though there was no snow on the ground in Nashua, the sky had been threatening it for several days.

"Frank," Shane said. "Been a while."

"It has." Frank smiled and nodded. "I'm sorry to stop by unannounced, but I was nearby."

"Not a problem. Come inside. Not a lot warmer, but I have coffee."

He stepped aside and Frank wiped his boots before entering and then removed his hat.

"You're not busy, are you?"

"Just watching a bird." Shane led them to the kitchen.

The triplets had vanished, as had Eloise and Carl. Only Herbert remained, and Frank was briefly startled by the large ghost's presence.

"Frank, this is Herbert. Herbert, this is Frank." Shane passed them both to pour a second cup of coffee.

"Hello," Herbert said happily. "Are you in the FBI?"

"Excuse me?" Frank asked.

"I've only met a few of Shane's friends," Herbert explained. "I'm not sure what everyone does, but Xander Ventura is FBI. Oh, and James Moran has a store."

"I take it you're new around here." Frank took a seat as Shane gave him the coffee and sat on the other side of the table.

"Relatively speaking," Herbert confirmed.

"Not an FBI agent, I'm afraid. Might need one before this is over, mind you."

"Problem?" Shane asked to keep the conversation on track.

"Seems like," Frank said. "I just came from visiting an old friend, Ted Raines. We knew each other in the service. He contacted me about his son Jackson."

Shane nodded and watched Frank add a spoonful of sugar to his coffee and stir it.

"Jackson haunted?" Shane asked.

Frank made a face like he was puzzling out the answer.

"Missing," he said.

"How old?"

"He's twenty-three. Bit of a free spirit from what Ted tells me. He didn't think there was cause for concern at first," Frank said.

"What changed?" Shane asked.

Frank held the hot coffee between his hands but did not drink.

"A letter. Jackson had joined what they call an intentional community. Like a hippie commune."

"Hippie haunting. Never seen that," Shane said.

Frank smiled weakly and offered a quick shrug.

"He was pursuing a girl, to hear his father tell it. College crush. It's an island near the Canadian border called Maple Grove. Jackson was sending his dad regular letters. I read a couple, and they're what you might expect. Wonderful place, great community, the robust feelings of a young man in love."

Shane grunted and drank his coffee.

"Then things changed."

"Yes," Frank agreed. "His final letter was shorter and clearly different. He was fearful that the island was dangerous. I read that as well. He details the beliefs of the islanders, the Elders of Maple Grove. How they worshipped this island spirit that provided for them, made the crops flourish, that sort of thing. He'd become convinced it wasn't just hippie stuff. That there was a spirit, but it was not looking out for them."

"He saw something?"

"He indicated as much in the letter but didn't explain," Frank said. "He said he needed to leave, and he'd be back home to see his father soon. Said he needed to pick his time because things kept coming up to delay him. And then there were no more letters. That was a month ago."

"No calls?" Shane asked.

"No phones," Frank replied. "The island is a self-sustaining rustic community. No phones, no internet, not even cars or electricity from what Ted says."

"Police?" Shane asked.

Frank nodded, finally taking a drink of the coffee.

"Ted called and got someone to investigate. They took a boat to the island, talked to the locals, and came back with nothing. According to the police, there was no sign of Jackson. Said the locals say he had left weeks earlier, headed back to Maine, and they hadn't heard from him since."

"But your friend isn't buying it," Shane said.

"Jackson kept in regular contact. The police decided since he has a history of wanderlust, he's in with these hippies, there's no sign of foul play, and his letter talks about a spirit and nothing 'real' as they see it, so he probably wandered off. They're not taking it seriously."

"Are we sure that's not what happened? Or that something bad just happened with some living problems? Hippies believing in earth spirits isn't a lot to go on," Shane said.

"I agree," Frank said. "Ted's not one to believe in anything he can't see. He only got in touch with me because he knows me and knows I investigate things that occasionally include missing people."

"But something brought you to my doorstep," Shane said.

"The letter Jackson wrote to his father. It didn't seem like anything concrete to Ted or the police, but there was a line in it about this spirit. He told his father he saw something, but that most of the others didn't see it. I don't know. It struck me that a ghost wouldn't be seen by most. But might be seen by some."

"So, if this kid is missing, what are you thinking? Ghost caught him before he could leave? Or these Elders?" Shane asked.

Frank shook his head.

"Sounds like they're working together," Herbert offered. "Like us at the carnival. Obviously, the people there know about it. Some of them, anyway."

Frank looked at the ghost for a moment, then Shane.

"Could be," Shane said. "What do we know about the island?"

"Little," Frank said. "There's a maple forest. The locals make syrup in small batches and sell it for a fortune on the mainland. Ted said they fish and grow some of their own produce. Make some crafty stuff otherwise. They seem self-sustaining and isolated. Couldn't tell me much more."

"We went to some isolated communities with the carnival," Herbert said. "Nothing like this, I don't think. But in Virginia and places, Appalachian communities, many years ago. It was like going to another world sometimes. When people isolate themselves that much, either intentionally or otherwise, they can turn to some very unusual practices and beliefs."

"Wouldn't be the first time I've heard about someone giving too much reverence to a ghost and things turning out badly," Shane said. "So, we go take a look around, shake some apple trees, and see what falls out?"

Frank smiled, and his attention shifted from Shane to the window.

Shane glanced back and saw Eloise slowly approaching the crow on the fence.

"It's an exciting day around here," Shane explained.

"I can see that," Frank said absently. He paused, watching the ghost and the bird, and Shane felt like the other man was stalling.

"Is there something else?"

"It sounds wrong," he said plainly. "Not Ted, but this island. You need to charter a boat to get there. They have no communication with the outside world. Even not knowing what Jackson said, this place sounds hinky to me."

"Hinky," Shane repeated.

"Very," Frank said. "No one sets up a place that can't be accessed without extreme measures unless there's a reason."

"So maybe Jackson's not the first missing person on the island."

"He is not," Frank said. "I only found one reference to this place anywhere when I researched it. It was the suspected site of a shipwreck, some fur traders in the late fifteen hundreds. Some researchers went looking for the wreck in the seventies but never found it, and it's just a footnote in their research. But there was a community there back then, fifty years ago. There have been people there for a long while."

"If they were all considered drifters, then perhaps many people vanished and were never reported," Herbert said.

"That's my fear," Frank said. "What if this island is a trap? An intentional one, and these people feed the needs of some spirit because they think it helps their crops? We would be walking into that with no way to escape."

Shane finished his coffee and shrugged.

"Wouldn't be the first trap I walked into," he said.

"You do lean into the more dangerous side of things," Frank said. "In that case, I'd like to formally ask for a favor. Will you come to Maple Grove with me and help me find out what happened to Jackson Raines?"

Shane looked over his shoulder and out the window again. He raised the cigarette to his lips and took a quick puff, exhaling slowly as he watched Carl discussing the crow with Eloise outside by the fence.

"Yeah. About time something happened around here, anyway."

CHAPTER 2

THE SEA

Frank seemed surprised that Shane was not just willing to go, but willing to go almost immediately. The truth was that Shane had felt restless lately. He had been home doing translation work and little else for weeks.

At first, it had been nice to not have the weight of a catastrophe or a living nightmare on his shoulders. He'd had enough close calls in recent history during which he barely managed to pull his ass out of the fire that getting a break from it all was welcome and maybe even well-deserved.

The problem was, after enough time of dealing with almost nothing else, just spending day and night in the house with the spirits that resided there, he fought harder and harder to concentrate on his work.

One day ran into the next in his mind, and the urge to just stretch his legs and do something grew. He wasn't inclined to up and go wandering for no reason, however. He wouldn't pull a Jack Kerouac and hit the road to experience what life handed him.

The weather outside was cold and only going to get worse. The house was like ice at the best of times, but winters always felt lonelier. Deader, if that was possible. It was as if the house welcomed the cold and desolation.

Maybe it did. The house was more tightly bound to the dead than the living and always had been. Shane was not sure if it was conscious and could think and feel like the ghosts, but it had instinct if nothing else. It leaned into death and cold. And he was just no longer in the mood for it. He welcomed a chance to be elsewhere.

Frank waited in the kitchen, chatting with Herbert, who was over the moon to have someone new to talk to. Herbert was a real people person.

It must have been the showman in him. They were really hitting it off, and Frank, apparently, had an appreciation for carnival life. Who knew?

Shane didn't waste much time. He packed a few things: clothes for colder weather and his iron rings. He debated for a moment whether he should go armed and then took his gun as well. Better safe than sorry, he supposed, especially if the locals were the sort to let a person die at the hands of a ghost. The gun would make a stronger point with them than an iron ring any day.

It had been some time since Shane had to deal with ghosts on their own. It seemed like far too often, the living were caught up in whatever was happening. Some were misguided, but they often knew what they were doing. Hell, sometimes, it was a business for these people. Making money off death. If not bartering and trading the dead, using them to get what they wanted from other people.

Sometimes, it was easy to forget where the dead came from. Every ghost was once a living person. Every horrible monster had roots in the living world. Sometimes, they were more similar than many cared to admit. And sometimes, the dead were far better people than the living.

Shane headed back downstairs. Frank and Herbert were laughing, and Shane caught the tail end of Herbert explaining something about the bearded lady and a drunk man outside of Tallahassee. He wasn't sure if it was a joke or an actual story about something that happened but was content to not know the details.

"Ready when you are," Shane said.

Frank nodded, letting his laughter trail off.

"We should get going, then. It might take some time to charter a boat," he said. He got to his feet, took his cup to the sink, and washed it.

"It was nice to meet you, Frank," Herbert said.

Frank put the cup on the drying rack next to the sink.

"You too, Herbert. Hopefully, we can talk more when Shane and I get back. I'd love to hear about your time in Fayetteville."

"I'm not going anywhere," Herbert said congenially.

Shane and Frank headed out of the house. Shane paused in the yard and let the others know he was leaving while Frank started his car. Eloise was unamused by Shane's decision to leave, but less so than she had been in the past. It seemed that even she could grow tired of Shane always being home. This would be a good break for everyone.

"Can we expect you to return home battered and half-dead?" Carl asked in German.

"I don't like to plan ahead," Shane replied. The ghost smiled and gave a slight nod.

"Stay alive, at least."

"Always do. Keep an eye on things," Shane said before heading to Frank's car. He dropped his bag in the trunk and then got into the passenger seat.

Frank's car had a very lived-in feel to it. The engine was loud, and the seats were cold. He had the radio tuned to a classic rock station that was playing CCR, and the heater chugged to warm the interior with cold air from the freshly started engine.

"Do you need to stop anywhere?" he asked.

"No," Shane said. "I have cigarettes."

Frank laughed at the comment even though Shane had not meant it as a joke. He shifted the car into gear and headed onto the road.

"Spruce Head is the closest port to Maple Grove Island," Frank said as they drove.

"Never heard of it," Shane replied.

"Not surprised. There are fewer than a thousand people there. I heard that's where the locals come in with their syrup, so it might be the best place to find someone who knows the way out. It's a little farther out than Matinicus Isle, but no ferry goes there since it's not an open community."

"How far off the mainland are we talking?" Shane asked.

"Twenty-five miles? Closer to Nova Scotia than Maine, I think, but still inside U.S. waters."

Shane said nothing. Twenty-five miles out to sea with no escape was precarious and stupid. If the island was full of people willing to kill to keep their secrets, or at least let a ghost do their killing, they would need to be careful. Maybe more tactful than Shane was used to.

Frank did not have much other information. He had the names of some people with boats for hire, but he had not contacted them. The ones he had contacted had shot him down, which made Shane question how likely they were to succeed with the people who hadn't answered the phone yet.

"Do we have a Plan B?" Shane asked.

"Not as such. But there are more than a hundred towns down the Maine coast with harbors and boats. There must be someone willing to make a few dollars, right?"

Shane had to laugh. That was technically a plan, but maybe not the best one. He was not skilled in chartering boats himself, though, so he didn't have a better recommendation. Frank's plan to hit up the closest town made the most sense, even if they didn't have any leads off the bat. If nothing else, they might find someone to give them some information about the island.

The trip up the coast to Maine took just less than four hours. The weather got worse the farther north they went, but it was still manageable. Light snow and some winds, but nothing that would impede their travel. That, of course, could change once they got out on the water.

Frank didn't talk too much on the trip. He wasn't reserved or sullen, he was just comfortable with the silence on the drive. Shane appreciated that. If he was with Xander Ventura, the FBI agent would likely have talked every free moment. There wasn't necessarily a problem with that, but sometimes, Shane just liked to cut to the chase.

Frank easily picked up on those kinds of vibes from people. He could transition from laughing about Tallahassee ghosts with Herbert to straight business talk with Shane and then let them both sit with their thoughts on the way to their destination. Shane saw why people hired Frank to deal with troublesome spirits in a less physical way than Shane would have.

Shane had met Frank on a case in a hospital some years earlier. Frank's path to his calling—dealing with the spirits of the dead—was far different than Shane's had been. The man had once been a monk and an army medic. He saw things with a far more sympathetic eye than Shane did. He also lacked the ability to physically fight a spirit if it came to that. In some ways, that meant he had to be more inventive and more adaptable. For him to survive an encounter with a spirit often meant being smarter than the ghost or finding a way to appeal to it in ways Shane never needed to care about.

That didn't mean Frank was a fool. He had called on Shane because he understood the danger. He knew he was heading into a situation where his skill set might not serve him as well as he needed it to. But maybe the two of them working together would prove more fruitful.

Shane had not asked Frank, nor was he aware if Frank had broached the subject with Jackson's father, about what condition they expected to find the young man in. Shane wouldn't speculate, but if experience was any guide, he didn't have a lot of hope for the kid.

If the islanders had something to do with his disappearance, whether a ghost was involved or not, there was little chance anyone would see him alive again. An island twenty-five miles from the mainland, in the middle of nowhere, was the perfect place to lose someone forever. Shane wasn't sure he would have taken this case if someone had approached him with it given the details they had.

There had been no definitive ghost sighting, and there was no definitive murder or kidnapping. The police had investigated and found nothing, and they were dealing with an island full of hippies. On its merits, Shane would not have thought much of it.

Shane trusted Frank's instincts enough that he had agreed to go despite his misgivings. Whatever Frank had learned from his friend had convinced him that it was worth checking out, and that was enough for Shane to give him the benefit of the doubt. If they were wrong, maybe the kid was fine and the island really was just full of a bunch of maple syrup-harvesting recluses. Maybe he and Frank would waste their time and nothing else. Shane could think of a lot worse things.

Outside, the snow fell in slow, fat flakes that were kicked up by the wind and swirled around the empty roads as Frank made his way toward Spruce Head. The little village was at the end of a long road that took them toward the looming, gray Atlantic Ocean.

It was midday when they arrived, but everything already seemed tired and sleepy. Few cars were on the road, and the handful of businesses they passed looked like they were either closed or not seeing a lot of customers. Shane had seen his fair share of small towns just like it. On a cold day, no one wanted to get out and do anything no matter the hour.

Frank drove slowly, winding his way down the narrow streets with only the general sense of wanting to get to the ocean in mind. Eventually, they found themselves on the last streets down which they could travel and the easternmost end of town, which led to a small harbor where several docked boats waited for them.

They parked near an office where Shane expected they might find the harbor master and got out into temperatures that were considerably colder than they had been in Nashua.

Shane looked at the ocean and the gray waves under a gray sky, rolling into shore. The horizon was blurry like a picture that someone had forgotten to finish drawing. Blank met blank, and it was like the end of the world. Wherever Maple Grove Island was, they would not see it for sure. It was right where the people who lived there wanted it to be, lost in nothingness.

CHAPTER 3

ONE WAY TRIP

The harbormaster was a short, stocky man with a bad attitude. When Frank asked him about getting to Maple Grove Island, he asked him if he looked like a cab driver.

"We need to charter a boat. That's a thing people do here, right?" Shane said.

"Boat captains handle their charters, not me. I'm just here to make sure you pay your fees and follow the rules in harbor. You want a ride? Go talk to someone out there."

He pointed out the door and then resumed reading a magazine. Frank sighed.

"Thanks for your help," he said.

The man grunted while the men headed back out. There were only about two dozen vessels docked in Spruce Head. Some were clearly fishing boats, most seemed like pleasure craft, and a couple looked a stiff breeze away from sinking.

There was a man on a small sport fishing boat not far from the harbormaster's who was taking some gear out of his vessel when Frank approached with a wave, with Shane trailing a step behind him.

"Hey there. Have a second to chat?" Frank asked.

The man was bundled up in a thick, wool coat and a hat pulled down to his eyes. He looked older than Frank, with a thick mustache.

"Sure." The man stopped his work.

"We're looking to charter a vessel. Wonder if you or anyone you know is taking on passengers?"

"I'm not licensed for it." The man shook his head. "But if you head down to the end of the slip, you might find Keith Danvers or Mo. They take folks out sometimes. You fellas looking to fish or…?"

"Looking to get to Maple Grove Island," Frank said.

The man on the boat winced, sucking his teeth audibly.

"That'll be a tougher ask."

"Why's that?" Shane asked.

"No one goes out there. They have a boat that comes in once a month, grabs some supplies, and sells stuff if they have it. They're a little… left of center, I guess."

"You ever been?"

"No, sir. No interest. Private dock, anyway. You can't just show up. You two don't seem like the type to head over there, if you don't mind me saying."

The man resumed moving his supplies around though he was still talking with them.

"In what way?" Frank asked.

The man on the boat chuckled.

"You know. Folks heading out there are a little granola. Usually a bit younger too, no offense. Guys from the boat, on the other hand… well, they're just weird."

"Weird how?" Frank got more curious.

The man slowed his work and looked from Frank to Shane and back.

"Just weird. Maybe a little quiet, you know? Reserved. Supposed to be hippies and organic vegan types, but they seem, you know… weird."

"Weird," Frank repeated. "I've been hired by a man whose son went to the island but hasn't been seen since. Hoping to get out there and ask some questions."

"You're a private investigator?" the man asked.

"Something like that," Frank smiled. Not an outright lie, but not entirely true. Shane wasn't going to question him.

"Like I said, I can't help, but they might. I'd try Mo if you're heading to Maple Grove. He's more likely to go that far out, and to that island. Most folks around here like to stick to buying their syrup and nothing else."

"Fair enough," Frank said. "Thanks for your time."

"No problem," the man said. "Mo's right at the end. Just saw him come in not twenty minutes back, so you should still be able to catch him."

Frank and Shane walked to the end of the dock where the man had indicated. They saw no one on any of the boats at first, but as Shane looked over a rough-looking older boat with a small cabin, a man popped his head up from below deck.

"It's quite chilly outside for a stroll, don't you think?" the man said.

"Looking for someone named Mo." Shane stepped back as the man climbed onto the deck.

The sailor looked paunchy, wore a too-tight sweater, and his hat barely covered his bald head. He had a wide smile that made him look friendly enough.

"You're looking for Mo, you found Mo," he said. Shane had trouble placing the man's accent. Middle Eastern, perhaps, but faint, and tempered with a touch of New England.

"We're looking to charter a boat and heard you might be able to help us," Frank said.

Mo's demeanor lightened, and he smiled broadly and nodded.

"I can do that, yes. Just tell me when and where, and we can work something out. I can take up to eight of you."

"Right now, if we can," Frank said. "It'll just be us. We need to get to Maple Grove Island."

Mo's smile stayed where it was, but he chuckled as he stared at Frank with a cocked head.

"Sir, come on now. I do fishing charters. You want to fish? I can take you fishing. I can take you to the Cranberry Isle. Casco Bay? Isle of Shoals?"

"Maple Grove," Shane said. "It's important."

"It's practically in Canada," Mo said. "And it is a private island."

"We know," Frank said. "I've been hired to find a young man who went there and has not been seen since. His family is worried."

Mo sighed heavily, his smile slipping away.

"That doesn't change the fact that it is still a private island. We're not welcome to dock there."

"What if you don't dock there?" Shane asked. "We just need to get there; you don't need to stay."

"Then you would be trespassing with no way to leave," Mo said. "That's a dangerous proposition no matter where you are, friend."

"No one has heard from this young man in weeks," Frank said. "His father needs to know what happened to him. This is the last place anyone knows for sure that he was."

"You need the police." Mo's voice was strained. There was some degree of sympathy, but his reluctance to go to the island was winning out.

"They went there. The people said everything was fine, so they left. No one is taking this seriously. They think the island people are just hippies and not worth worrying about. But this man—his name is Jackson—has people who love him. People who deserve to know what happened to him."

Mo let loose another sigh that sounded almost like a growl. He turned away from Frank and Shane and looked at the ocean, watching the gray skies, and rubbing his head through the hat.

"This weather is not good. Getting worse. There are a lot of rocks around the island. Treacherous passage in poor weather. If you go there, you might be stuck. For days."

"Then they'll have to talk to us," Frank explained.

"Unless there's funny business, hmm?" Mo countered. "You play a dangerous game."

"At least it's a game we're volunteering to play," Shane said. "This kid didn't have a choice."

Mo continued staring at the sky over the ocean as though the clouds were telling him something only he could hear. Shane knew he was wrestling with himself but didn't want to face the others while he did it.

The desire to not get involved in someone else's problems competed with the desire to help because he had the ability to do so. Shane had wrestled with it more than once himself. He couldn't fault the man either way for whatever he chose to do, but it would make things easier if Mo could drop them off and leave. He wouldn't be putting himself on the line too much by doing that.

"You can leave right now?" Mo asked.

"We can," Frank said. "Our bags are in the car."

"Get your bags." Mo wasn't happy about it. "I can drop you off on this island, but you are asking for trouble. There is no communication. No way out if you get into trouble."

"We'll manage," Shane said.

He stayed with Mo while Frank returned to the car to get their bags out of the back. Shane helped the man remove some of the bumpers and lines from his boat as Frank returned, tossing their bags on the deck and hopping on board with them. They were ready to head out in a matter of minutes.

"Give me your names," Mo said.

"Frank Benedict and Shane Ryan," Frank said.

"Good." The captain raised a cell phone and snapped a quick picture of them. "I have your names and pictures. I will wait a day and if I hear nothing, I will tell the police you went to the island and vanished, yes?"

"Three days," Shane said. "Give us three days."

He looked at Frank, and the other man nodded. If they found nothing in three days, they probably wouldn't find anything.

"Three days," Mo repeated.

They worked out compensation quickly, with Mo not driving as hard a bargain as Shane expected for a last-minute trip to a place he didn't want to go. He was very accommodating given that he wasn't staying, and it seemed clear he expected something bad to happen.

"I feel like you know more about this island than you're telling us," Shane said once they were underway, heading slowly past the harbor markers and out to sea.

"You think I'm keeping secrets?" Mo asked from the helm with a laugh.

"Maybe not secrets, but the first guy we talked to had some opinions about the island. Made it seem like everyone avoids it for more than just the privacy concerns."

"Hmm," Mo intoned. "I know what anyone in Spruce Head knows. They make syrup. It's expensive but good. They come to town maybe once a month. They are not friendly."

"No one thinks that's weird?" Shane asked. "Tree-huggers who are standoffish?"

"Island folks are tough by nature," Mo said. "In the Caribbean, you relax. Here? You fight. It's harsh here. So maybe the people have to be harsh. They choose to live a harsh life on that island. No electricity, no phones, just them against nature, year-round. Especially now, in the winter, it gets very hard. So maybe that takes something out of them. Makes them... I don't even know how to describe it. You don't feel welcome. They don't come across as friendly, welcoming people. I'm not sure how their community works, but I know it's not something I want to be a part of."

"Do you think they're dangerous?" Shane asked.

They had left the harbor and were now out on the open sea. The water was choppy, but not dangerously so. Mo's boat, though older, had powerful engines and made simple work of getting through it. He had set a course to a bearing that looked to be in the middle of nowhere.

"Who isn't dangerous?" Mo asked. "Under the right circumstances?

Not for me to say."

They continued course while the captain made small talk, mostly with Frank. Shane saw some smaller islands early in their voyage, but soon enough, there was nothing but water all around them. Finally, a shape emerged through the murk as they approached Maple Grove.

The place was much larger than Shane had expected. As they got closer, he saw a substantial forest and the rocky edges of the island that rose to dangerous cliffs. It gave the island the effect of looking like a bowl from a distance.

"Here," Mo said, once the docks were in sight. The island's dock was much smaller than the one on the mainland. It looked like a simple wooden platform with three boats moored in place. A snowy path next to it led up a hill and vanished into the island. "Look here."

The captain was not drawing their attention to the island but to the radio near the helm of his vessel. He pointed to the digital readout, tapping the red number sixteen with his finger.

"Channel sixteen. You call for Mo within three days. If I don't hear it, someone else will. This is always monitored for emergencies. These boats all have a radio on board. You call for me on channel sixteen when you need to leave."

"Sixteen, got it," Frank said.

Mo hit the radio again with his finger, the nail making a clicking sound on the numerical display.

"Sixteen," he said again.

CHAPTER 4

THE FROZEN PATH

Mo stayed just long enough for Shane and Frank to disembark and then wasted no time leaving the island. Shane saw the rocks Mo had warned them about as the boat headed back to the mainland. As the water rose and fell, crashing against the cliff faces of Maple Grove Island, smaller jags of stone were exposed like stony fingers from the deep. If any boat got too close to the wrong part of the island, it would likely be gutted.

There was nothing to be done about it now. Mo had gotten them where they needed to be, and he was off. Shane tossed his pack over his shoulder and looked at the boats tied up along the small dock at Maple Grove.

Two of the vessels were small fishing boats, and the other was barely more than a dinghy. But Mo had been correct, each of them—even the sad little dinghy that couldn't have carried more than four passengers—had a radio on board. If push came to shove, they could get back to the boats and get a signal out.

With no phones on the island, Shane assumed the radio was the only way the locals communicated. There might be radios further inland as well. He doubted any phones would have worked so far from shore, even if someone were secretly holding them. Maybe a satellite phone, but from what he'd been told, this didn't seem like the sort of people to have technology like that.

Shane saw nothing of interest on any of the boats, just the sort of things one would expect. Someone had left several partly empty bottles of alcohol sitting out on one. The other of the larger two boats had boots and a coat on deck, but there was no sign anyone had recently been there.

"What do you think?" Frank joined Shane at the last boat.

"Big." Shane looked up at the island.

He wasn't sure what he had expected, but Maple Grove was an impressive size. He was surprised no one else had claimed it and a settlement years ago. Maybe the proximity between Canada and the United States made it an inhospitable stop. The hills and cliffs didn't look welcoming, and the rocks offshore would also be a hazard.

Those were, of course, rational concerns and questions. If the island was what they thought it was, then that was the answer. Ghosts had a way of poisoning land. A haunted house could sit empty for generations. Realistically, the real estate would be valuable. Someone could have torn the place down and built a new house, a shopping mall, or a car lot. But people with aspirations like that often lost their enthusiasm once they spent time in the place. Even if they never encountered the ghost, the land had been spoiled. It put people off like a feeling they could not shake, making them not want to stay.

In a harsh and remote spot like Maple Grove, if the land was haunted, it would be easy to come up with excuses to not go there, build there, or turn it into a resort community.

"Guess we follow the path," Frank suggested.

The path up the hillside switched back on itself and was covered in a thin layer of snow. From the sea, there had been no indication of where the town might have been.

"I don't imagine anything is paved under that snow. Watch your footing," Shane said as they headed out.

"Paved." Frank laughed. "I was in the Army, you know."

"I know," Shane said. "That's why I said it."

Frank laughed as their boots left wood for snow-covered soil. Shane had no personal animosity against the Army, and certainly not against Frank, but as a Marine, if he couldn't bust Frank's chops a little bit, he wasn't doing his job.

The frost crunched underfoot as Shane led the way up the hillside. The path's zigzag pattern ensured an easy climb but not a fast one. He assumed it was designed to ease the locals when bringing carts of syrup down from up top, or bringing supplies up from the docks, but it was a lot of wasted energy. Given the unfamiliar terrain and the weather, he also didn't want to risk a shortcut straight up.

By the time they reached the top, Shane was breathing hard and watching it puff out in front of his face in misty clouds. The cold seemed stronger even though the elevation was hardly remarkable. The sky above was as grim as ever, and the wind had picked up. Heavy, clumpy snowflakes whipped toward his face from the open sea to the east, and there was a harshness to the wind they hadn't felt below.

Ahead of them was open countryside. There were scattered trees, and to the left, they grew dense and became a full maple forest, seemingly devoid of all other tree types. To the right were snowy plains with some irregular trees and skeletal shrubs among hills and valleys. Far from them, maybe a half-mile inland, smoke rose in thin wisps. It was the only sign of civilization, but it looked like quite a hike with the terrain.

"There's nothing here," Shane said.

"Maple trees. Maple syrup. Snow. And our village of hippies. Did you expect more?" Frank said.

Shane shrugged.

"Not really."

"If there is a ghost, it's got to be focused over there." Frank pointed to the smoke from the town.

"Unless there's more than one," Shane suggested.

Maple Grove was a decent size. With so much space, one ghost could not cover the entire island on its own. But when Shane surveyed the landscape, it was clear that the remoteness, especially that time of year, wouldn't do anyone any favors even if they got more than a mile from the spirit. The forest looked like it extended to the far end of the island. Being stuck in endless woods in the snow was not the most welcome alternative, especially for someone who wasn't prepared for survival.

Shane started in the direction of the smoke. There was no visible trail now that they were at the top of the hill. The snow blanketed everything evenly and hid whatever paths the locals followed. They had not bothered to build roads from what he saw, and he could only imagine the struggle to carry goods to and from the boats. It seemed like these people wanted to make life hard. Their ideal of a simple hippie commune did not compute in Shane's head based on what he saw.

"Not sure what I was expecting." Frank trudged at Shane's side. "But this was not it."

They walked for a short time, struggling to maintain proper footing over the treacherous landscape. Shane was apprehensive as they headed toward the village to consider what they were dealing with. If they needed to run for any reason, they would be seriously hobbled. The snow made it impossible to see where they could step or where they could not. He and Frank had already sunken into small pits or stumbled on roots that they couldn't see.

The wind was picking up out of the east. The ocean air was bitterly cold, and it brought a noise with it. At first, Shane thought he might be hearing a person or a spirit moaning in the distance. But the longer he listened, the more it became clear that the wind was passing through some of the rocks along the face of the cliff. There must have been caves or tunnels that funneled the wind and made the noise.

It droned on, producing a very low pitch like a death rattle from the island itself. Shane wondered if the locals even heard it anymore. It was the sort of white noise that might fade into the background after enough time.

"Very low-frequency," Frank pointed out. "That sort of sound has been blamed for hauntings."

"I've heard," Shane said.

Some scientists had concluded that winds traveling through an old stone castle made the same low-frequency sounds. If they were low enough, even below the register a human could hear, they caused all kinds of sensations including the feeling of being watched, nausea, and paranoia. Of course, a ghost could do all that and more. All things being equal, people should be so lucky to be haunted by a low-frequency sound and nothing else.

Shane had seen nothing moving on the island during their voyage. There were no animals; not even birds had bothered to roost there. He suspected the weather was keeping things like gulls at bay, but it was interesting that there were not any tracks in the snow to indicate small game or even mice.

More interesting to Shane was that there were no human tracks, either. The people of the village had not been to the dock in at least a day, maybe longer. The snowfall was not heavy, so any old tracks would not have been too covered up. The locals were simply not venturing out.

"If Jackson had been out here, there would be no way to track him," Shane pointed out, though it didn't really need to be said.

He was working through the scenario in his mind before they reached the village. It made sense to keep an open mind, but based on what he had heard, he didn't expect a warm greeting with helpful citizens.

If the police had correctly relayed the information, the islanders had told them that Jackson had left long ago of his own volition. Assuming that he had not just neglected to mention leaving to his father, there was no way that was the case. They would have to work from the assumption that Jackson was still on the island and that they would get no help to find him. If anything, they might be working against the locals.

"This is your show. How do you want to approach these people?" Shane asked.

The walk from the boat was longer than it should have been. Half an hour to cover just the relatively small distance, and Shane felt it in his legs by the time the little village was in view in the valley below them.

"Honestly," Frank said. "We're here on behalf of Jackson's father to find out where his son went. We don't need to be confrontational even if their story doesn't mesh with what we know. If they insist that Jackson left, we can say that no one saw him after this place, and that's why we're here. It's the truth, and it'll make it easier to keep any story we have straight."

"Fair enough," Shane said.

Shane didn't think it was the wrong approach. He would have told Frank if he thought there was an issue. It might not have been Shane's choice of approach, but Frank knew what he was doing, and Shane trusted him enough to be smart.

The village was in a bowl in the island, surrounded by a slight ridge all the way around. From above, the place looked like an image from a Christmas card: little handmade log cabins with snow-capped roofs and chimneys billowing white smoke. Shane counted maybe four dozen houses, and a couple of other buildings might be for storage or meeting places.

Everything in the village was built around a central hub. From the outside, it presented as an open space with a podium or altar in the middle of it. It looked like stone, but Shane couldn't make out the details.

A stream ran along the eastern edge of the town and filled a pool at the southern end. A farmland sat beyond the town, and Shane saw small gardens and a modest-sized greenhouse, the most modern thing on the island next to the boats.

Shane and Frank descended from the edge of the bowl, down the shallow edge toward their destination. The two men were nearly in the village before any of the islanders made themselves known. A tall man dressed in thick pants and a long wool coat left one of the houses, heading up the road to somewhere deeper in the village. He didn't look back to see

Shane and Frank, and they did nothing to make themselves known.

"Think there's a town hall, or do we just start knocking on doors?" Shane asked as they entered the town, heading down the first unmarked street between buildings.

"Hey!" a voice called out. Shane stopped with Frank at his side as a man emerged from the first house. The man held a hunting rifle that looked like it pre-dated World War II. It was pointed at Shane's head. "Who are you?"

CHAPTER 5

THE VILLAGE

Frank already had his hands up while Shane was slower to do the same, though he didn't raise them nearly as high as he turned to face the man pointing the rifle.

Snow swirled around him, and the man's nose and cheeks were red. He was thin and bony but very tall. He had a pronounced Adam's apple and a pointed chin. He reminded Shane of stories of Ichabod Crane but bundled up for the winter.

"My name is Frank Benedict." Frank took a tentative step toward the man but kept his hands up. "I was hired by a man named Ted Raines to find his son Jackson. Did you know him?"

Ichabod looked pensive. His barely restrained fear and anger faltered a bit, and now, he seemed unsure. Shane was close enough to have taken away the man's gun without any trouble, but instead, he stayed where he was and waited to see what came next.

"He's not here," the man said. "We told the police everything."

"I understand," Frank said, "but his family still hasn't seen him, and this is the last place he was spotted. We'd like to talk to you and whoever else might have had contact with him. See if he said or did anything that might explain where he went."

Ichabod wavered. It was obvious from the man's demeanor that he was not used to decision-making around town. He had come out by chance because he had seen Shane and Frank, no other reason. He lowered the weapon in his hand and glanced between the men unsurely before shaking his head.

"You need to talk to Mallory," Ichabod said. "She knows more about it all."

"Good. Great. Can we maybe do it without the gun?" Frank asked.

"Oh."

The man did not seem sure how to proceed, and Frank turned his wrists so that his hands were out instead of up in a more pleading manner. After a second, Ichabod nodded and then placed the gun back inside the doorway of the house he had come from.

"Sorry, it's just… you know. Sometimes, people come who don't belong and cause trouble."

"Sure," Frank said. "You need to protect what you have here. Can I ask your name?"

Shane had lowered his hands and pulled a cigarette from his pack. Frank was ready to handle everyone with kid gloves, so Shane figured it was best to put something in his mouth and keep it busy so he didn't cause them trouble. For now, anyway.

"Clint," the man said. "My name's Clint. I didn't mean to scare you fellas, I promise. I never even shot that gun."

"I understand, Clint. You're just being responsible; keeping an eye on your home. Water under the bridge," Frank smiled as he told him.

"Yeah, okay. Mallory lives up here, near the greenhouse." The tall man led the way.

Shane inspected the houses as they traveled. Some were very sturdy, but others were almost ramshackle. Some were a mishmash of wood and scraps of metal, panels, timbers, and wrought-iron decorations or painted pottery and gnomes. One house was almost completely bedecked in wind chimes made from glass, old cans, bottles, and silverware. They hung from every edge and surface that would hold them.

Other people ventured out of their homes as Shane and Frank were led through town by their guide. Several called out to Clint to ask what was happening, and he told them that newcomers were in town, and he was taking them to Mallory.

A few of the people who came out waved at Shane and Frank and even welcomed them to the village. Frank waved back or said hello, and Shane nodded at anyone who made eye contact. Once again, his expectations did not line up with reality.

Aside from Clint's off-the-cuff reaction with the gun, everyone seemed like what they should have. They were hippies. They lived in hippie houses, and it looked like they did hippie things.

Clint led them to a quaint house next to the greenhouse. Unlike many of the others, this one was assembled from stones and looked extremely old. Shane guessed it was built in the eighteen hundreds if not earlier. The tiny windows were made of thick, hazy green glass, and the sky-blue door had a knob in the center. The tall man knocked.

"Is Mallory the mayor of the village?" Frank asked.

"We don't run like that. She's the highest of the Elders, so you could think of her that way," Clint explained.

There was a rustling from inside the home. After a moment, the big, wooden door swung inward to reveal an elderly woman in a bulky, wool dress. Mallory was barely above five feet, and her long, flowing white hair was tied into a substantial ponytail. She wore a pair of thick, fur-lined boots and a scarf.

Her eyes darted from Clint to Frank to Shane, who was standing behind them, and then back to Clint.

"Clint, I see we have some guests."

"They're here about Jackson," Clint said. "I overreacted when I saw them come into town and pointed my rifle at them. I was just... with everything going on—"

"It's fine, Clint. You owe these men an apology, not me," the woman said.

"It's fine," Frank said. "We talked on the way here. I'm Frank Benedict."

He held out his hand, and the woman looked him up and down briefly before accepting.

"Mallory," she said. "Welcome to Maple Grove Island. I have to say, we don't typically like getting visitors without an invitation."

"Of course. Unfortunately, we weren't sure how to contact anyone here, and time is of the essence. We're looking for Jackson Raines. I understand he might have lived here, and no one has heard from him since his stay."

Mallory nodded and exhaled into the cold. People in the village were gathering around, whispering, and no doubt making up stories. She stepped back into her doorway and invited them in.

"Clint, do you mind telling everyone we just have a couple of visitors and that there's nothing to get worked up about?"

"Sure, Mallory." He bowed his head in an oddly obedient fashion.

"Come on in, please. Get out of the cold," she said to the other two as Clint left.

Shane closed the door behind him after stomping his boots clean of snow on a small mat out front. Mallory was already bustling off in her small but very cluttered open home to the kitchen, where she filled a kettle and then hung it over an open fire.

"Tea will be ready in a few minutes." She invited both men to sit at the small, square table by the fire.

A single hallway led to the back of the home where Shane suspected a bedroom and perhaps a bathroom waited. The rest was a big, open space ringed by stone and the misty green windows.

Shelves, cabinets, hutches, and drawers covered every inch of the walls, and Mallory's house was packed to the ceiling with stuff. She had bundles of dried herbs hanging from the rafters, jars of maple syrup, jars of unidentifiable objects and fluids, and dozens and dozens of books.

"I'm sure Clint told you, just as I told the mainland police when they came here before, that Jackson didn't stay with us for long. I don't think the young man's heart was in it. The hard work, the commitment… some people think life out here is a cakewalk, just smoking weed and loafing around all day. That's not how we do things."

"So, Jackson didn't have the work ethic you need for a place like Maple Grove?" Frank asked.

Shane added nothing to the conversation, which was clearly preying on Mallory's nerves as she shifted her gaze to him every so often. Frank, however, was a natural when it came to a calm and smooth interrogation. The cops could have taken lessons on demeanor and tone from him.

"No. Nor the ethos. We are here to work with nature as one. A symbiotic union. The land, the trees, and us together in harmony. Jackson was not ready to submit to something like that. He's too rooted in the world we chose to leave behind."

"Of course; he's still very young," Frank said. "What can you tell us about the day he left? Did he share his plans? Where he was going? What he wanted to do next?"

Frank was talking almost as though he'd rehearsed the dialogue. Mallory took it in stride, but answering questions with lies caused her to pause more often.

"I am not aware of his plans beyond returning to the mainland. I thought he said something about Canada, but I'm afraid I didn't spend much time with the young man."

"Who did?" Frank asked.

Mallory stared at him as though she didn't understand the question, and then the kettle she'd hung over the fire began to whistle, distracting her briefly as she rose to fetch it.

"Everyone tries to be welcoming here." Mallory poured hot water into Frank's cup and then Shane's. "Everyone probably spoke with him at some time or other."

"There was a girl," Shane said, speaking for the first time. Mallory made eye contact with him as she filled her cup and then set the kettle

40

aside on a small hot pad.

"Yes," she admitted. "Alina. She was the one who invited Jackson to the island."

"He probably spoke to her more than anyone else then, do you think?" Shane asked.

Frank sipped his tea, and Shane felt the tension coming off the other man. Shane smiled and took his cup, having a sip as well.

"You're probably right. She would likely know his state of mind better than anyone here, and where he might have headed when he left. I can have someone show you to her home so you can speak with her when you're ready."

To her credit, Mallory was not rattled. Not that Shane was explicitly confrontational, but he was curious about how she would react to them knowing about the girl. The older woman maintained her composure. Either this had already come up—maybe when the police were there—or she had planned how to handle this. In any event, her calmness showed that she wouldn't easily be caught off-guard.

Even though she hadn't tipped her hand, and there was still no real reason to believe anything sinister was happening on the island, Shane's gut told him something more was going on than what they could see. Clint's near explanation to Mallory about why he had the gun meant something. The faint tension at the corner of Mallory's eyes, especially when she looked at Shane, told him all he needed to know. Maple Grove was hiding something.

"We just want to find Jackson. This is the last place anyone can confirm him being. I really do apologize for the intrusion, but I appreciate your willingness to help," Frank said.

Mallory focused her attention on him once more. She smiled, and it was warm and grandmotherly, and Shane saw how most people would have believed it. Tension still wrinkled the corner of her eyes, though. There was still stress there, even in the set of her jaw. She didn't like them being there and asking questions.

Good, he thought. *Let's see how long you can keep up your game.*

"Of course," Mallory said. "Even though Jackson did not fit into our community, he was a very likable young man, and none of us here bear him any ill will. Anything we can do to help you, we will do. Do you know how long you might need for your investigation?"

Frank nodded, sipping his tea again before setting down the cup.

"Obviously, we don't want to intrude more than we have to. But for this kind of sensitive work, when someone is missing, and especially given the state of the weather, which will slow us down, I was thinking at least a day or two, if that's acceptable to you."

Mallory blinked with the teacup at her lips. She faced Frank across the table. Shane sat off to the side, able to see them in profile. He watched as her jaw tensed and flexed. He said nothing and did nothing. He knew before she spoke that she would agree to it even though she did not want to.

"Yes, certainly," she agreed. "You can stay in Jackson's old cabin for the night. We have communal meals in the Great Hall, and you are welcome any time."

She set her cup back on the rough, handmade wooden table and casually got to her feet. Shane set his cup down as well, and he and Frank got to their feet to be polite.

"I have a lot to do today, especially to make sure you both have what you need, so forgive me, but I must get to it. Please, if you don't mind, go find Clint again. Tell him I asked him to take you to speak with Alina, and you can keep me up to date on anything you learn. Sound good?" she asked.

"Wonderful," Frank said. "And very appreciated. If we learn anything, you'll be the first to know."

He extended a hand, and Mallory shook it. Shane smiled and nodded, and the men headed toward the door. Shane opened it and saw himself out, while Frank paused for another word of thanks.

After the door closed behind them, both men stood in front of her home in the cold air. Shane pulled out a cigarette and offered it to Frank.

"You know I don't smoke," he said, looking at it.

"You sure?" Shane asked. "Thought you might need to replace all that smoke you just blew up her ass."

Frank tried not to laugh.

"Keep your voice down. Let's go find Clint."

CHAPTER 6

THE GIRL

Most of the people who had come out to marvel at the two strangers had disappeared again. The weather had gotten colder. The wind was a bit stronger than it had been, though the snow had not yet arrived. Even in a heavy jacket, Shane felt the wind cutting through.

He pulled a simple, black stocking cap from his pocket and put it on to keep warm. He had been out in enough remote locations in the freezing cold to know better than to brave the weather like a fake tough guy. The last thing he wanted was to have a snowstorm be the end of him.

"What do you think?" Frank asked when they were a short distance from Mallory's home, heading back toward Clint's cabin.

Shane glanced at him and slipped a cigarette between his lips.

"She's lying." He lit the end between cupped hands to keep out the wind.

"I agree," Frank said. "She seemed unnecessarily tense. Her answers were almost practiced."

"But she's confident," Shane pointed out. "She's going to let us stay here and talk to people. That means she doesn't think we'll find anything."

"Could be that she just doesn't want to raise more suspicions by denying us. It's not like this is a government office with an expectation of privacy and security. They need to live up to their philosophy here. Can't do that by keeping us away."

"Maybe," Shane said.

He didn't believe it. Based on what Mo and the other captain had said on the mainland, the islanders were awkward and standoffish. They might have thought they were welcoming, but their actions were perceived differently.

They reached Clint's little cabin and before Frank could knock on the door, it opened again and the tall, skinny man was there. Thankfully, he'd left the gun inside this time, and he looked out nervously at them.

The house behind him was dimly lit. Shane could only make out the front room, but it was very cluttered and smelled heavily of herbs and maple.

"Is everything okay?" Clint asked.

"Yes," Frank said. "Mallory has invited us to stay in Jackson's old cabin while we're here. And she asked if you could show us around and take us to speak to Jackson's friend Alina."

"Oh, sure," Clint said.

He took a scarf and some mittens off a rickety table near the door and stepped into the cold with them. "Alina's probably home right now. She's been pretty down since Jackson left. She paints sometimes, and I think she's been doing that."

Clint led them down the same path they had just traveled twice now but continued onward through the little village. It did not look like anyone had planned out Maple Grove. The streets, such as they were, were haphazard and took strange twists and turns to get around cabins and other buildings that had just been built wherever.

Some structures nearly touched, and others were yards away from everything else, surrounded by footworn paths and muddy grass peeking through the snow. There was little coherence in any of it. Some houses didn't even seem to face the streets they were on, and they were at odd angles to one another.

It was clear that the village had endured several periods of growth. All the oldest stone houses had a similar look. Later, someone had built the log cabins, which were clustered together. And then after that, there was a third wave, which seemed to be the biggest. These were the least skillfully done homes, the most ramshackle and confusing of the bunch, and they were everywhere.

Shane guessed that the most modern homes were the ones made by the current residents of Maple Grove. The previous structures, made of timber and stone, must have been from early settlers on the island. They looked extremely old. Even the log cabins looked like something from more than a century earlier.

Clint took them down a narrow, muddy path to one of the farthest houses in the village, close to the southern tip of the island. This one looked quaint like a tiny house Shane had seen that people could order on the internet.

There were brightly colored decorations outside, though the smattering of snow diminished some of the charm of the aluminum sunflowers and wrought-iron toads that lined the walkway to the emerald-green front door.

"This is Alina's place." Clint stopped at the end of the walkway. "I'll be around when you guys are done, and I can show you to Jackson's place or we can get lunch or whatever you like, okay?"

"Sure, Clint, that's appreciated," Frank said.

Clint had a strange innocence to him, now that he didn't have a gun in his hand. There was something vaguely childlike about the way he conducted himself and in the unsureness in his voice. Shane had misjudged him, but a rifle did that sometimes.

Frank approached the green door as Clint dawdled off, looking back a few times before he vanished back into the village. Frank knocked and waited while Shane finished his cigarette, exhaling smoke into the increasingly harsh wind.

They stood in the cold and silence, waiting for Alina to answer, but no one appeared.

"Must be at the grocery store." Shane looked around. "You want to go shmooze the locals?"

Frank shifted his feet and nodded.

"Looks like she's not around. Sure, yes, let's go see who else around here might know something about Jackson."

Shane had turned his back to Frank and the house and was looking down the next street to their right, where they had not yet been. A man stood outside of his home, one of the more rickety structures covered with panels of corrugated aluminum, smoking what looked like a corn cob pipe.

When Shane approached, the man pulled the pipe from his mouth and exhaled a cloud of lavender-colored smoke that had an odor Shane couldn't identify. From beneath a bushy, gray beard, the man smiled.

"Afternoon," he said.

"Hey," Shane said. "We're looking into the disappearance of Jackson Raines. You know him?"

"The young fella." The man took a long draw off his pipe again and nodded. "Sure. Stayed a few days and then headed back to the mainland. Wasn't to his tastes, as I understand it. Never talked to him much."

"You know anyone that he spent much time with here? Or maybe more about what he did while he was here?"

The man shrugged.

"Sorry. Like I said, never talked to him much."

"Sure," Shane said with a nod of thanks.

Frank took the lead with the next person, a woman in her early forties with blonde dreadlocks held back under a hat. He did his friendly introduction routine and then delved into some questions about Jackson. What kind of person he was, why he might have left, friendly banter. The answers he got were as minimal as the ones Shane had gotten. He seemed like a nice young man. She never talked to him much. She didn't think he fit in and didn't know anything else.

The wind continued to kick up and more snow fell, whipping down the irregularly sized streets between cabins and shacks throughout the village. Shane and Frank approached at least a dozen people who were congenial and not particularly evasive, but also not informative in any way.

Each of the villagers spoke of Jackson in mirrored terms. He was nice. He didn't seem committed. He left. Again and again, another version of the same story. If the townspeople were to be believed, Jackson spoke to almost no one in any detail for the entire time he was there.

"This is going well," Shane said once they had freed themselves from a couple in one of the stone cabins who had nothing new to add but hoped they found news about Jackson soon.

He was smoking another cigarette, and his hands were cold. He had gloves, but he had yet to fish them out of his bag. He hadn't been expecting to wander around the town so long, listening to people tell them the same non-story again and again.

They had decided to track down Clint and maybe get a more guided tour when a woman between two houses stopped them.

"Hey." She looked both exposed and furtive in her attempts to seem casual and stealthy.

She was young and very pretty. Her eyes were green and her hair, under her hat, was a bright and vibrant red like polished copper. There were small braids at her temple, brushed behind her ears, and laced with beads and small shells. She had to be Alina.

"Did Jackson's dad really send you?" the girl asked.

"Ted's been a friend of mine for years," Frank said. "He wants to find Jackson."

Alina looked Frank in the eye, and then quickly glanced at Shane before looking back. Her eyes darted from them and scanned the street on which they stood.

"You need to check the woods. Past the tapped trees. It's snowed a lot; I don't know if you'll see anything. But you need to look. And then you need to leave."

"I promised Ted—"

"It's not safe here. For you. I mean, I don't think so. We can talk more later, maybe. Did you come here on a boat?"

"We were dropped off," Frank explained.

The girl's expression became fraught.

"When are they coming back?"

"We have to make a call."

"God." Alina grimaced. "It's not… no one here's going to help you. Please. Go past the tapped trees in the deep woods and then call your boat."

"Can you tell us what we're looking for in the woods?" Frank asked.

He kept his voice low, but the girl looked frustrated by the question and shook her head, looking down the road in both directions again.

"I have to go. Please, just leave as soon as you can," she said.

She turned her back on them and headed away quickly, not bothering to look back. In seconds, she had turned past one of the houses and was gone. It didn't seem as though anyone was around, but that didn't mean no one had heard or seen them together. She was trying to be quick and inconspicuous.

Shane and Frank looked at one another when she was gone, Shane taking another long puff from his cigarette before he started down the muddy road toward Clint's house.

"You figure we get quarters first and then head out?" Shane said.

"Sounds good," Frank agreed.

They needed a place to stay if they planned to sneak off into the woods in search of whatever might be waiting out there. The girl's information was limited, but at least she told them something new. Shane had seen the forest on the way in, and there was a lot of ground to cover. Heading past the tapped trees wasn't the best direction he'd been given, but it was the only one they had. He hoped she would have said more if there was something more to say.

Clint was on the street just outside his house, talking to two other men. The trio quickly parted ways as Frank and Shane approached, the two mystery men giving them some sidelong glances before they disappeared to parts unknown.

The veneer of friendliness in the town was still there, but it was losing some of its shine. The repetitive answers and glances they got from everyone they weren't talking to spoke volumes about the greater mystery that no one did a good job of hiding.

"Did Alina have any helpful information?"

"She wasn't home," Frank said. "But we were hoping you could show us to Jackson's place. It's cold out here; we could use a rest to warm up before we find anything more."

"Sure. Winters on the island can get very bad," Clint agreed. "We get snow drifts bigger than the houses; you don't want to be caught in that."

"Sounds like it," Frank replied.

"Come on, I'll show you the cabin," Clint said.

They headed down the same road once again.

CHAPTER 7

THE ALTAR

Clint took them to one of the log cabins near the end of town where they had first entered, not too far from his place. It had a sturdy build to it, and the cracks were well filled with a mixture of clay and sawdust.

It was a simple building on the inside, and fiercely cold. Frank set about starting a fire after Clint showed them where everything was, and then the taller man left them to make themselves at home.

The cabin was not spacious. There was one bed and one cot. A small dining room table had two chairs, and there was a tiny kitchen area with a fireplace.

Shane looked through the cupboards and the small closet. There were few supplies left in the building, and nothing to eat, just tea. He and Frank had picked up basic rations before leaving the mainland, enough to sustain them, but they planned to take Mallory up on her offer of meals until the offer was rescinded. They expected that to happen sooner rather than later.

Nothing in the cabin looked suspicious. Shane looked for a listening device or a camera, something that countered the apparent simple lifestyle of the people in the village, but there was nothing. If Mallory and her people wanted to spy on them, it seemed they would do it the old-fashioned way by listening at the door.

Frank had the fire started quickly. It would take some time to fully warm the space, but it was small, and they had a good store of wood. If they had planned to stay in the cabin overnight, they would have been comfortable.

Shane took a seat at the table, folding his arms over his chest, and

Frank joined him. The fire warmed them as they sat in silence, listening to the howling of the wind outside.

"I didn't expect any honest answers," Frank said at last, "but the reactions seem unusual. There's no real animosity. None of these people seem hateful."

"Don't need to be hateful to kill," Shane said. "Especially if you think you're doing so in service to a greater cause."

"You think they sacrificed him for their island? For maple syrup?"

"If a ghost told them too, maybe. How old you figure those stone huts are?"

"Very old. Hundreds of years," Frank said.

"Could be a ghost that's been in this place a long time, got a whole shtick. Good at manipulating people. I think we should talk to Mallory again, ask her about Jackson's letter. What he thought about what they did here."

"I think you're right. We might need to turn up the heat a little, but I don't want to get exiled before we've learned everything we can the friendly way. Maybe we can get a look at that altar in the middle of town," Frank suggested.

The village was arranged around the center hub, but they had not stopped to check it out yet. The paths they traveled were circuitous and had avoided it. The townspeople seem to avoid it, too, circling it instead of heading directly to their destinations. But since they had been given leave to roam about and talk to people, surely no one would mind.

"Won't learn anything in the cabin." Shane gestured about in a general way. "If Jackson stayed here, they cleared it well after. No sign anyone's been here in ages."

"This fire won't have the place warm for some time yet, anyway. Might as well head out for round two," Frank said.

"Sure, why not?" Shane agreed.

They left their bags behind, minus anything Shane felt was important.

If someone broke in and went through their stuff, all they would find was clothing and food.

He wore his gloves and hat this time and was thankful for them the moment they opened the door. The sky had darkened even though it was still only midday. Thick, gray clouds had rolled in from over the ocean and hung low and menacing over the island. A storm threatened to break out at any moment, but so far, the wind was only whipping around a light scattering of snow.

The duo took a side street that cut right through the village and made their way to the center. What Shane saw from outside of the bowl of the valley on the way into town was exactly what he expected it to be.

It looked as though someone had set up a sort of wagon-spoke effect at one point, with the stone altar in the town square as the central hub and the streets as spokes leading off. But as with everything in Maple Grove, additions had thrown off the balance, and now, part of the wagon wheel was crooked and warped.

Shane was not sure if the central stone—a tall, narrow pillar—was meant to be a small altar or some kind of speaking podium. The surface had been ground flat, and it was about chest height. There was a slight angle to it so someone could have put a book on it, maybe to read to a crowd, but it was not significant.

"Not as significant as I had hoped." Frank inspected the pillar.

There were no markings on it, and no stains beyond what years of sitting there in the open air had done. No sign that it was anything more than a chunk of useless rock.

Maple Grove was wearing on Shane's patience. The thin trail of breadcrumbs they followed was not leading anywhere, but something was obviously below the surface. He couldn't fault Frank for playing it safe, but that had run its course in record time.

"Mr. Benedict!"

The voice came from behind them and Shane turned, startled, as

Mallory approached them at a quick pace for a woman of her years. "Please; you can't be here."

She had her arms extended in the way a grandmother might usher her grandchildren back into the house after playtime. Shane raised an eyebrow, and the woman was forced to slow her pace and put down her arms.

"We were just having a look at your stone," he explained.

"This is our Gathering Place. It is for ceremonies only. We don't tread on the land here except for when we give thanks to the land."

Shane looked down at the ground. Sure enough, despite his and Frank's footprints, and now Mallory's, the snow was unmarred in the circle around the stone pillar. No one had walked there at least since the snow had started to fall. It would have been much easier to travel across the tiny village by heading through the middle, but it was small enough that going the long way was not much of an inconvenience.

"This stone have some significance?" Shane asked, putting his hand on it.

Mallory let out a sound, something between a gasp and a frustrated sigh. She wasted no time reaching out, taking Shane's hand, and pulling it away from the stone.

"This is sacred to us. This stone has been with the land for centuries. It channels the will of this land. Please, come away."

Frank and Shane shared another glance, and Shane saw some distress in Frank's eyes. He didn't want to make this an issue so soon. Shane joined him, leaving the small altar with the old woman, out of the central circle, without protest.

"You must understand, for those of us who choose to remain here season after season, this land is like our shepherd. It watches over us and protects us, but we must also protect and care for it. That is the cycle we have dedicated our lives to. We give to the land; it gives to us. On and on, for all our lives."

"How do you do that?" Shane asked.

Mallory led them back toward their little cabin, but the question gave her pause.

"I'm not sure I understand the question," she said.

"What do you give to the land?"

"We make sacrifices every day. The sacrifices of our labor and dedication. We cherish the land and give praise to it, for it is our Mother and Father. To understand, you would need to be one of us."

There was a hint of acid in Mallory's voice for the first time. Just the faintest bit of strain, impatience, and maybe even anger. It was still well-masked. If Shane was pushing her buttons, it was a very slow and subtle process, and she handled it well enough.

"Please, gentlemen. You are welcome here for the duration of your investigation, but I must ask that you respect our ways. We'll be having dinner in three hours. Join us in the main hall then. Everyone will be present, and you'll be able to speak to anyone and learn whatever you can there."

"That sounds like a good idea," Frank said.

They stopped outside of the cabin they had just left with a clear but unspoken suggestion that they stay home until dinnertime. Though shorter than both men, Mallory tried to be imposing as she stood in front of them, drawing herself up and keeping her gaze locked on Frank's eyes rather than Shane's.

"I understand that you want to find Jackson. I wish you well, but you will not find your answers here. Please ask what you need to ask and be on your way. This community is meant to be self-sustaining. We don't need or want the outside world with all its problems here. I keep this place running for the good of us all, and we can't do that with disruptions."

She spoke like someone who was used to being listened to. The grandmotherly feeling Shane got from her before was even stronger now. She was a matriarch, and it was expected that when she said "jump", they would do it.

"I understand," Frank said.

"Do *both* of you understand?" Mallory turned to Shane. "Your friend seems a little less interested in preserving our peace, Mr. Benedict."

"I'm all for peace," Shane said. "We'll be out of your hair as soon as we get what we need. Promise."

Mallory looked unconvinced. Shane said nothing more, and the older woman nodded after a moment and then returned her attention to Frank.

"Someone will come and get you when the meal is ready."

Frank's words of thanks met her back as she walked away, this time heading toward some buildings they had not approached.

"I believe we have been scolded," Frank said when she was out of earshot.

"That altar has to be something," Shane said.

He hadn't noticed anything in particular when he'd touched it, but the weather was far too cold to tell if a ghost might have rooted itself to the altar. Either way, Mallory was far too protective of a plain piece of rock in the middle of a dirt circle.

The wind continued to whip snow into their faces. They had reached a roadblock as far as the townspeople were concerned. Shane was ready to follow Alina's directions and head into the woods. Better to head out now before the impending storm.

"You look like you're hatching a scheme," Frank said.

Shane laughed.

"A scheme? You're too into your character."

"Am I wrong?"

Shane shook his head, turning to look out of town and back the way they had come.

"I want to head out there now. We still have some light, dim as it is. Give these people a rest from their schemes, whatever they are."

Frank nodded, and the wind ripped the steamy breath from him as he exhaled.

"I think I'm going to try to talk to the villagers some more. Split their focus if anyone sees you leave, plus I can still hit up the communal meal if you don't make it back in time."

"I shouldn't be more than a few hours. Let's meet back here then, compare notes after," Shane said.

"Good luck," Frank said.

Shane pulled out a cigarette and nodded.

"Watch your back."

The path out of town was already obscured by newly fallen snow, so Shane forged a new one while Frank returned to town.

CHAPTER 8
SECRETS

Frank lifted the cup and took a small sip of tea. If he drank any more tea in the village, he would spend the rest of his day in the bathroom. Since he'd left Shane to investigate the town and talk more directly with people, every single one of them had invited him in for tea. He was on what must have been his tenth cup. None of it was particularly good.

Shane's presence was more than appreciated, and Frank had a distinct feeling that when push came to shove, Shane would be invaluable in getting to the bottom of whatever had happened to Jackson Raines. But when it came to simple conversation and being friendly with people who were disinclined to want to be helpful, Shane did not have the most tact.

On his own, Frank did what he did with any investigation. He talked to people. He couldn't throw punches across the spectral plane and knock out a poltergeist. All he could do was communicate and hope people could see where he was coming from, or at the very least let something useful slip.

Frank didn't doubt that the people of Maple Grove were keeping secrets. The answers he got initially were far too rote and practiced. His inclination was that Mallory told people what to say should anyone arrive. They'd probably come up with their story before the police came the first time, so everyone was well-practiced and comfortable by the time Frank and Shane showed up.

Simple lies were easy to tell. All anyone had to remember was that yes, Jackson had been there. No, he was not there anymore. If anyone like Frank wanted detail, they shrugged it off. They didn't know him well.

Frank knew that the problem with telling lies was that they were hard to commit to. Like a scab, the more you picked at one, the more you revealed underneath. And if you did it in a friendly enough manner, people didn't even know they were exposing anything.

Frank was sitting in a cozy, wooden cabin with a couple that were about his age. Miriam was an artist who worked with pottery. Her partner—not her husband—was Neil. He was something of an organic farmer who was responsible for the greenhouse in the village.

Like every other place Frank had seen in town, Miriam and Neil had an eclectic group of decorations in their home. Brightly colored pottery pieces covered nearly every flat surface, a testament to Miriam's artistic eye. To her credit, many were very beautiful, and under other circumstances, Frank might have even considered buying something from her if they were for sale.

"You have a great sense of color." Frank nodded to a small vase in the center of the table that was a brilliant cerulean.

"Thank you," Miriam said. "It's hard to source good cobalt stannate to make it, but I mix all my pigments."

"Really? That's fantastic. You can tell when an artist puts in the effort, I think. It really makes a difference in the finished work."

"Oh, definitely," Miriam agreed.

They sipped their tea, and Frank nodded.

"It's funny, Jackson's father told me he had no eye for art. That's why he was surprised Jackson came to stay here."

"He was really more into the gardening," Neil pointed out.

Miriam smiled and nodded.

"Because of Alina, obviously."

"True," her partner replied. "Girl has a way with peppers. Biggest, sweetest peppers we ever grew in that greenhouse. Jackson tried some tomatoes, and he tended them well, but tomatoes practically grow themselves."

"He was good with them, was he?"

"I'd already planted them before he got here, but he kept them looking good," Neil said. "He was a good kid."

An awkward silence fell over the couple. Neil lowered his eyes for a moment and cleared his throat while Miriam focused heavily on her tea. Frank was moved to ask how long it takes for a tomato plant to grow if Jackson was only there for such a short time the way everyone had initially said, but he kept the question to himself.

"I'll have to let his father know he has a green thumb," Frank said with a smile, finishing his plain, slightly bitter tea.

"Yes," Miriam said. "Let him know Jackson was a bright spot in our community. A lot of us have been here a bit too long; got a bit too stagnant. It was nice to have some youthful energy."

Neil and Miriam nodded at the sentiment, and Frank got to his feet.

"You've been gracious hosts, and I thank you for your time," he said. "If you can think of anything else, please let me know."

"Oh, so soon?" Miriam said, sounding disappointed.

Frank shrugged apologetically.

"I don't want to take up too much of your time. Yours or anyone's. Still more people to talk to, but you've all been very welcoming and forthcoming."

It was only mildly underhanded and manipulative to use politeness as a weapon. Frank wanted the people he talked with to feel bad about lying. It wasn't a tactic that would work on bad people, but that was not the feeling he got from the residents of Maple Grove. Instead, he felt like he was confronting a community that was in over its head and didn't know how to get out.

He needed them to regret keeping secrets. He wanted them to feel guilty about not telling him what happened to Jackson. Even if no one broke and exposed the full truth, they would be more inclined to let things like the tomato story slip. Jackson had been in the village longer than

Mallory had said, and that was confirmed now. Frank just needed to keep picking the scab.

If there was a ghost on the island, if it had killed Jackson and the people of Maple Grove knew about it, guilt could be a powerful motivator to get someone to point Frank in the right direction.

The fact that the spirit worked with people, or at least seemed to, meant there was a chance that Frank could work something out if people would start telling him what he needed to know. The ghost couldn't have been a senseless killer if it allowed the villagers to stay where they were. It must have had a need or a motivation. If it had even semi-rational motives, Frank could talk to it and maybe work something out. He just needed someone to crack.

He left Miriam and Neil and looked around the village. The snow was coming down harder, and the sky was darker. He saw smoke coming from the longhouse-style building where Mallory had indicated they would eat their meal. The cooks must have been in the kitchen getting everything ready.

One thing Frank had learned in the Army was that getting to know the cook is vital. Cooks inevitably see everyone's face a couple of times a day. The people making dinner must have gotten to know Jackson at least a little bit.

Frank cut across the village, avoiding the center of town and the altar, and let himself into the longhouse through a set of heavy, double wooden doors. Several braziers were lit inside, keeping the building warm. They were placed evenly down the left and right side of the building, on either side of two long tables set with benches.

There was more than enough room for everyone in the village to sit and eat at the same time given the layout of the place, but no one was there in the front area.

Frank made his way to the back through a doorless frame into a large kitchen area with two fires burning and a trio of chefs chopping vegetables and chatting among themselves.

"Saw the smoke from outside and thought you could use a hand," he said, recognizing two of the three people in the kitchen from previous chats in the day.

"The more the merrier," a woman named Grace said.

The group was making beef stew. Frank wasn't sure where or how they kept meat on the island. They had no livestock, nor did it seem likely they had any refrigeration that would have lasted in the warmer months. Maybe they didn't keep meat in the warmer months.

He helped the cooks wash and peel carrots and potatoes and then chop them up along with some onions, green beans, and shelling peas. They browned the beef in the big pots, then sauteed the onions and other vegetables, getting a nice caramelization before starting on the broth. Frank made polite conversation the whole time.

"Mallory told us a bit about the spirit of the island," he said casually, dicing some more carrot. "And some of your beliefs. The cycle and such."

It was hard to say much without sounding like he was fishing for information. But they were just having a friendly conversation, and he hoped no one would think any more of it than that.

"It's tough here." Grace nodded. "You need to have the grit. We've lost people in past winters. You see how cold it is now? This is nothing. With no hospital, and no easy trek to one, some people don't make it. We have to keep our minds and hearts in order."

"You lose people?" Frank asked.

"Oh yeah," another woman, Laura, said. "Lost Carl and Paulina last year. Lovely couple but frail. All part of the cycle."

"The cycle," Frank repeated.

"Happens all over the world, Frank." Grace smiled. "Life begets death begets life. We come here and put our sweat and blood into the soil. The soil gives us these beautiful vegetables and the syrup that sustains us. It's just nature. The way it's supposed to be."

"I suppose you're right. Nature gives and takes," Frank said.

"Way of the world," Grace agreed. "The lives given here nurture those left behind. Everyone who calls this place home knows that. We take it to heart. Give unto the spirit, and it gives unto you."

"Sacrifice," added the third cook, a brusque man called Ned. "It's how it works. We've all seen the results."

Frank chopped his vegetables in silence. Their words sounded cultish like people conditioned to believe and spout the same ideology. More importantly, they sounded as though they believed that death was not just normal but required. He wanted to believe that they were referring to the cyclical nature of life and death and metaphorical sacrifice, but circumstances did not allow him to give them the benefit of the doubt.

He couldn't ask if Jackson had become a sacrifice to the island, but he also couldn't shake the thought. These seemingly friendly, gentle people might have murdered a young man in the misguided belief that it was what the island wanted. That it was even a good thing.

"Can I ask you all a strange question?" Frank moved to the fresh peas.

"No question too strange around here," Grace said with a chuckle.

"I was just thinking… You were talking about the spirit of this place. Not so long ago, I was in a place—a hospital—and something was there that I didn't understand at first. People died there like here, but the spirit in that place…"

He trailed off, tossing loose peas into a bowl.

"What about it?" Grace asked softly.

"Nothing. We're making dinner; I don't want to sound like a strange fool crashing your hospitality," Frank said.

"Nonsense," Laura said. "We're all friends here."

Frank smiled and nodded.

"I think the spirit in that hospital was a real thing, not just an idea. Is that crazy?"

There was silence for a moment, broken only by Ned's gruff grunt.

"I don't think that sounds crazy," Grace said after a moment.

"They're real," Laura reassured him. "Don't doubt that for a second."

The silence picked up again and lingered for a long moment while they finished chopping the vegetables. Frank dumped his carrots and peas into one of the big pots and helped stir with a long, thick wooden spoon. The group moved on to other topics, and Frank didn't want to bring it up again. He didn't need to.

He had seen the glances among the other three. The way they concentrated on their work and then looked at one another before they replied to him. All three were thinking the same thing; he saw it plainly on their faces.

The ghost in Maple Grove was a real thing. And whether they had done it willingly, he was certain the people there had killed for it.

CHAPTER 9
IN THE WOODS

Shane was breathing heavily by the time he reached the top of the bowl. The cigarette had been a bad idea and did not last long before he pinched it out and returned it to the pack. Between the physical exertion of fighting his way uphill through the snow and the whipping wind, finishing a stick wasn't going to happen.

Once he had reached the top, it was like walking through a door into a new, worse place. It was the difference between experiencing a storm through an open window and stepping outside into it.

The wind was stronger, colder, and much less forgiving without the protection of the little rise around the village. He pulled up his collar and his hat down. Ahead, across the island, the forest of maple trees looked like a wall of shadows. Some still had red or yellow leaves stuck to the branches, but they were few and far between. In the blasting wind and snow, he doubted many would last much longer.

There was no indication anyone had paid attention to him leaving the town, though he wouldn't bet that he wasn't being observed in secret. Either way, he wasn't doing anything forbidden. No one had told him not to leave the village. No one had told him not to inspect the woods.

It was not a great distance from the edge of the village to the maple forest, but the open field between them was unusual. The fact that there was any space in a place with no roads or trucks made it seem like they were making more work for themselves than they needed to.

Although it was covered in snow, something about the size of the empty space between the village and the forest tickled something at the back of Shane's mind. Just an open area between the two. It made him think of two forces meeting on a battlefield. The village on one side, the forest on the other. The space in the middle—the place where Shane was walking—was no man's land. That was where people went to die.

The wind gusted, the snow flurries became heavier, and Shane's field of vision got smaller as a result. It was hard to see what waited on the horizon.

From where he stood, ankle-deep in the snow, Shane couldn't even see the path they had taken up from the ocean. He strained his eyes, and for a moment, he thought he saw something there. The shape of a person, a gray silhouette against a gray background. Something... someone familiar. A woman.

It was just a shadow. One of the distant trees. But for just a moment...

How long had it been? They were in Maine. He hadn't thought about it, hadn't allowed himself to. Maine was where it had happened. Where he'd lost her.

Jacinta.

No. Just a shadow. The longer he stared, the clearer it became. Just his mind and the weather playing tricks. There was no time to let his thoughts wander. Frank was counting on him. This kid's father was counting on him. He had work to do.

Shane pulled up the collar of his coat and finished the slow, deliberate hike across the snow plains to the forest's edge. The tightly packed maple trees offered cover from the onslaught, and the snow on the ground between them was not as deep or dense. It made the walk easier, and he was glad for it, even if he lost more visibility because of it.

There were no tracks here, either. No sign of squirrels, rabbits, or any woodland creatures one might expect in such a forest. The snow was still freshly falling, so maybe nothing had had a chance to come out yet. Or maybe nothing was alive in those woods but the ancient trees.

Metal spigots pierced the trunks of every tree he saw, with half-covered aluminum pails hanging from each one to collect the dripping sap. It was an old-school way to harvest, and surely more advanced methods were available now, but the people of Maple Grove stuck to tradition.

He lifted the lid on one of the buckets and looked inside. A pale, clear liquid sat about an inch deep in the bottom with bits of bark and a leaf floating in it. He wondered if it was too cold to collect the stuff, or how long it would run out of the tree.

Every tree around him was the same. Hundreds of spigots and pails hanging off tree trunks, slowly collecting the lifeblood of the maple. They extended as deep into the forest as he could see. Surely, they didn't have the whole forest tapped. That would be thousands of trees. Could such a small community process that much?

Shane wasn't sure how much sap was needed to make a bottle of maple syrup. He knew it needed to be boiled down and concentrated. If the townspeople were doing the whole forest, they had a bountiful harvest. Given the price of maple syrup, the people of Maple Grove probably made a good living despite the way it looked.

Shane had learned that among the many reasons to fall in with a dangerous spirit, money was often at the top of the list. If these people thought a ghost was the reason they were able to harvest sap and make money, they might do anything to preserve that. Even kill a man.

Alina had given no indication about what Shane was supposed to be looking for in the forest. He ventured deeper. There was no path laid out, nothing to indicate where other people commonly walked before him, so he stayed on a northern track, moving between trees as necessary.

The ground was covered in leaves, some dry enough to crunch underfoot. Shane weaved past countless dented, well-used-looking aluminum buckets of sap until he reached a part of the forest where the trees were not tapped.

A short distance ahead, he saw a clearing through the trunks, a space of pure, white snow with no growth. There was no movement, but the dim light and multiple trees could have hidden anything. The clearing would be a good spot for an ambush, but it was the only thing Shane had seen since he'd entered the woods that looked different.

He approached slowly, making as little noise as he could. He made his way closer from tree to tree, watching the clearing and the surrounding forest for any sign of movement. If something lay in wait, it was still as a statue and out of sight.

He paused two trees away from the clearing, crouched behind the thickest tree, and waited. The clearing was no more than twelve feet across and mostly circular. Something was there in the snow, maybe stumps or rocks, but they were obscured by the snowfall, so he could not say for sure.

The wind that moaned through unseen caverns along the eastern face of the island sounded mournful and tired. Its wails were long and deep, and they mixed with the rattling of skeletal branches that clicked and clacked when the gusts grew strong enough.

Shane's breath had no time to cloud before his eyes. The wind stole every exhalation from him, scraping its icy fingers across his face while he stayed still and silent. He waited patiently for five minutes, then ten. He felt the cold seep into his boots and through his gloves.

Slowly, Shane crept forward. He entered the clearing and scanned the surrounding forest. Nothing presented itself, so he walked into the open toward the hidden objects beneath the light smattering of snow. He used a gloved hand to wipe off the nearest one, pushing the snow aside to reveal a stone slab.

Nothing was remarkable about the stone. He pushed the snow aside, expecting to find little beyond the stains of age, but as he wiped it clear, he made out a faintly inscribed cross filled with white flakes. He traced the cross with his finger. It was crudely done, probably by hand with a knife or ax blade scraped back and forth.

A second stone was hidden beneath the snow a short distance from the first. A similar cross was inscribed on that one as well. Shane worked around the clearing, wiping off more stones, each bearing a nearly identical cross. Some were more smoothly done; some were a little larger or a little deeper. If he had to guess, they were not done at the same time or with the same tool.

Shane paused after he cleared the seventh stone. It bore an inscribed cross like the others, but the stone was not as plain. The gray rock had been stained. It looked black now, but the color was unmistakable. Blood had been spilled on the stone long ago and left to set, probably in much hotter weather. It had stained the surface, seeped into the porous material, and remained there as a part of it. Not just a few drops or a splash. Enough to have cost someone their life.

The clearing was a graveyard, but not for the people of Maple Grove. Shane felt this was older. The stones had been there for a very long time, and the carvings predated everyone living on the island. Maybe not the stone huts, though. Those original inhabitants could have used this area to bury their dead. The blood, he suspected, was not that old. Not new, but not that old.

The plainness of it reminded him of the altar in the center of the village. Very nondescript, almost like an afterthought but still meaningful. The simple headstones were like that.

Still, if this was what Alina had meant for Shane to see, he didn't understand her message. The blood on the stone could not have belonged to Jackson. There was no sign among the rocks that the young man had been there. There was no sign of anything recent.

The howling wind picked up again, blasting through unseen caves. Still crouched over the bloody stone, Shane's eyes scanned the forest again.

Blowing snow and shadows upon shadows cast by the trees obscured so much. His eyes scanned from the left to the right, looking for any sign of the young man, the people of the village, or anything.

A flash of red next to a tree trunk caught his eye, low to the ground and mixed with the snow and exposed dry leaves. It was too bright in color and too vibrant against the dull backgrounds of the snowy forest. Fresh, flowing blood set against the backdrop of pale flesh.

The ghost crouched next to the tree, on even footing with Shane. It had been some time since he had seen anything quite like the spirit that stared back at him. Large chunks of flesh were missing from the dead man's body. The legs especially, bent into a crouch like a frog ready to hop were almost clear of meat. Ragged bits dangled from the underside of two exposed femurs. The tibias in front were no different, with the calf muscle excised on one and slashed almost in two on the other.

Someone had skinned away the ghost's cheeks and lips. All the wounds looked fresh as though they had happened just moments earlier. The spirit stared at Shane, meeting his gaze with wide, bloodshot eyes that looked manic. Shane realized it was because they were lidless, unable to blink, and fixed on him so intently.

Neither Shane nor the ghost said anything. With a quick clatter of its teeth like a nervous gesture, the ghost ran.

Not away, but toward Shane.

CHAPTER 10

THE FROZEN DEAD

The ghost was heading toward Shane like an animal, swift and nimble. The lack of muscle on his bones did nothing to hinder him. He seemed single-minded and predatory, focusing solely on the living man.

His first attack seemed to surprise them both. Shane expected the ghost to come at him full-bore, ready to kill, and unaware that Shane could fight back. Instead, the spirit moved low to take Shane to the ground. It was not an attack someone made when they felt they had an advantage, and as a result, Shane was not quick enough to defend against it the right way. The fact he *could* defend had caught the ghost off-guard.

The result was the two of them grappling. With cold, clammy, meat-encrusted bones in his hands, Shane forced the ghost's arms away to gain the upper hand. The ghost felt slick, and it made him hard to hold on to. Not a sound escaped the spirit's lips, or what remained of them, anyway. He was more silent than the forest itself.

Whenever Shane got a grip on him, the ghost contorted himself and slipped away, his slick bones slipping between Shane's fingers. He used his broken form to his advantage, twisting away from Shane so Shane could not hold tight.

At no point did the ghost slow or hesitate in his attacks. Whatever Shane threw at him, the ghost improvised and immediately countered. By the same token, the ghost couldn't get the upper hand over Shane. He tried several moves, including what appeared to be submission holds, all of which Shane countered. Their fight became a wrestling match in the snow, a battle of moves and countermoves with no one coming out on top.

They struggled through the snow-covered tombstones. At one point, Shane planted a booted foot firmly in the ghost's groin and launched him backward. He landed silently, not making a mark in the snow, then twisting around onto his hands and knees like a cat ready to pounce.

Instead of attacking, the ghost slowly backed up on all fours, his eyes locked on Shane. Shane crouched next to the bloody stone, ready to meet the ghost if he came back at him but content to catch his breath.

Despite the freezing temperature and increasing wind, Shane had worked up a sweat fighting the spirit. He knew it was dangerous to get so hot in the cold. Even if he won the battle, having clothes soaked with sweat in the freezing cold was a death sentence. He wondered if the ghost had considered that. It was an insidious strategy if he realized what was happening.

"You don't have much to say." Shane felt a freezing tickle of wind work its way down his spine.

Predictably, the ghost had no reply. Shane could not gauge his thoughts based on expression since the spirit had so little flesh left on his face. There was no way to tell if he was enraged or if this was a game.

The ghost came for the second round with more caution. He was fast but not frenzied, understanding who he was up against now. Shane's face and throat were the targets this time. Shane was ready as well and countered more easily. He adapted to fight the slimy, thin limbs, focusing instead on the meaty parts.

When they were in close quarters, Shane saw that the ghost's bones were marred by cuts and gouges. Someone had taken a blade to the spirit, but it wasn't the sole source of the dead man's wounds. There were teeth marks along the radius and ulna of the right arm. Human teeth. Someone had bitten through flesh and bone more than once.

Mangled flesh bits were harder to discern, but Shane saw teeth marks in some of the less cleanly cut flesh. The ghost had been at least partially eaten. If the wounds were on his spirit form, there was every reason to believe it had happened while the man was still alive.

Shane tried to snap the ghost's right arm. The elbow joint was exposed, and it should have been an easy, crippling blow. Instead, the ghost jumped and twisted in midair, undoing the strain Shane had placed on the arm, getting behind him, and pushing the living man to the ground face-first.

Before the ghost capitalized, Shane rolled and scrambled out of the clearing, deeper into the forest. He put trees between himself and the ghost and staggered to his feet. He needed the ghost unbalanced and at least a few seconds behind in predicting where Shane would go.

The ghost clambered after him, darting around and then through trees, unencumbered by physical form. The chase was short, and Shane was in his clutches again, taking a dive down a small embankment toward an ice-covered stream.

With no need to worry about his own well-being, the ghost collapsed on Shane and forced him to keep rolling out of the snow and onto the ice. The island was cold but not cold enough, and the icy layer was too thin. It cracked under Shane's weight, and he and the ghost plunged into the freezing water.

Skeletal fingers pulled at Shane's clothing, and his body reacted to the shock of the water, causing him to gasp involuntarily and draw in a breath. Water filled his lungs and seared his insides as every inch of him was rocked by a sudden onslaught of brutal numbness.

Then rage overcame shock. Shane was not going to die in a stream in a maple forest, the victim of poor physics and planning. The stream was shallow, and he pushed up as hard as he could, dragging his waterlogged body and the ghost up with him.

With a fierce growl pumping adrenaline through his freezing body, he lifted the ghost out of the stream and threw him to the bank. The ghost hit the snow, and Shane climbed out on the other side, water pouring from his clothes.

The wind was still whipping through the trees and pelting him with snow. Saturated as he was, Shane had only minutes to get back to the village or someplace warm before hypothermia set in.

He thought about how long it took him to get to the clearing once he had stopped investigating the area. He had been slow, he had stopped to observe more than once, and he had taken a meandering path to look around. He had left the village several hours ago.

At a straight shot, Shane guessed it was maybe a fifteen-minute run. Fifteen minutes to get back to the village. Maybe twenty minutes?

Shane pumped his legs, forcing himself through the snow. It wasn't deep between the trees. The forest had prevented a great accumulation, so he made better time. As fast as he could run in wet clothes that were icing up, anyway.

He looked behind him and saw nothing. The ghost had vanished. It was no longer next to the stream but not pursuing him where he could see it, either. There was no time to care about what was happening with the half-cannibalized spirit.

Shane pushed forward. He couldn't feel his feet, and his teeth chattered. A dullness crept into his mind, and he struggled to focus as he pushed himself to run as fast as the uneven ground allowed, forcing himself to move and keep as warm and on task as he could.

The clock was ticking.

✳ ✳ ✳

Frank stood alone in the cold, adjusting his gloves. Shane had not returned, and their small cabin was undisturbed. Dinner would begin shortly. Everything had been prepared for the stew, and it was coming along nicely. Frank had excused himself to go see if Shane had discovered anything.

Snow was falling more heavily, and the wind refused to relent. The sky was also darker than it should have been. The clouds above were ominous, and the threat of a storm loomed closer than ever. Frank was certain it would snow overnight; it was only a matter of how much.

Shane had planned to be back within a few hours. That was an indefinite time frame, but Frank was uneasy. Shane should have been back by now. Maybe it was just paranoia, or maybe it was intuition, but Frank adjusted his scarf and gloves and then headed out of the village and up toward the plains of snow.

It was hard to keep his eyes open and search properly as he walked with the snow hitting his face. He had thought he'd find Shane by catching sight of him, sure his friend would be visible when he got close enough, but the blowing snow created whiteout conditions in the open field. He barely saw the forest ahead of him. The cliffs that led to the sea might as well have been on another world.

Frank pressed onward, reaching the tree line after struggling through banks and gullies created by the blowing snow. It was easier to navigate inside the forest. The trees offered a significant blockade to the weather, and Frank felt like he was walking on the ground again, not just piles of wet muck.

There wasn't much to see other than the numerous aluminum buckets full of sap. The persistent snowfall, even within the trees, meant there was no trail to follow.

Frank did not believe that he possessed any special insight, but his instincts were not bad. Though he didn't put a lot of stock in luck, it had come through for him more than once. He chose a direction and started walking, searching for signs of where Shane might have gone or anything that could have happened to Jackson in the woods.

Snow and leaves crunched, and the wind howled. The deeper he walked, the more he noticed a smell blowing in from the east, something subtle but hard to ignore. Something was rotten, if only just.

Frank headed toward the smell, and it grew stronger. The cold and the wind should have prevented it, but the repugnant odor of rot became thicker. It was not natural.

Nothing looked unusual among the trees, but he slowed his pace and slipped his hands out of his gloves to expose the iron rings he wore on each hand. If something in the woods was teasing with the scent of death, he did not expect a friendly encounter.

Frank's foot slipped, and he caught himself on one of the trees as he nearly fell into a narrow gully that had been hidden by the snow. Leaves and detritus rolled down from under his boot as he righted himself. The stink of decay caused him to raise his free hand to his face.

Below, in a small ravine like a crack in the earth, a pile of dead bodies barely touched by the snow sat pale and damp. The size and shape of the ravine shielded it from the blowing winds like a naturally formed grave set on either side by tree roots that held the earth in place and created a protective wall.

The gap was filled with numerous bodies piled upon one another. Those at the bottom were skeletal and old, but the newest body on top was nearly fresh and preserved by the cold weather.

Frank saw it was a young man, face-down, stripped of his clothing though bits clung to the wrists and ankles in ragged scraps. Great chunks had been torn from the body, especially along the legs and arms where it had been reduced to bone. The man's ribs were exposed across his back, and part of his scalp had been torn away.

One hand was exposed, atop the head of another corpse, the fingers splayed and stained red. Frank saw a ring there, a simple one made of silver with an engraved pattern. He recognized it from a photo he'd been given. Even with the face turned away, and the body ravaged, Frank recognized the young man he had never met.

He was standing over the corpse of Jackson Raines.

CHAPTER 11

THE STORM

Shane stumbled out of the tree line and nearly fell into the open field of snow. The wind whipped at him and cut through his clothes. He might as well have been wearing nothing for all the good the wet garments did.

He held himself tightly as he walked, teeth chattering and the biting sting battling with the numbness threatening to overtake his body. He growled and let the sound grow louder, forcing adrenaline through his veins to push himself.

Nothing pursued him out of the forest. The ghost was gone, and his absence nagged at Shane. The spirit had the advantage after the fall into the stream. Shane would be dead now if the ghost had pursued him. Instead, there was simply no sign of him.

Shane was not one to look a gift horse in the mouth and was not going to argue about the opportunity to escape with his life. He was still not safe by any measure.

The sky was dark, with the last vestiges of daylight swallowed behind the thick cloud cover that blew in from over the ocean. The snow pelted him at a forty-five-degree angle, and it was coming in thick, messy clumps rather than individual flakes.

Shane forced his legs to work. He could barely feel anything below his knees. His thighs were tight, and the material stretched over them cracked when he moved due to the ice crystals that continued to set. He would not stop because he could not stop.

There was nothing to see once he was beyond the tree line. Ahead of him, and soon behind, was just a whiteout.

He could not see the village ahead of him, but he had an idea of how far he needed to travel. He stuck to that, keeping his head low and his body as small as he could to conserve heat until finally, at long last, he saw lights.

He focused on the soft, yellow glow. Candles or lanterns in the windows of the houses in Maple Grove. When he reached the edge of the bowl that surrounded the little town, he slipped and lost his footing, falling all the way down to the unpaved road next to one of the stone cabins.

Getting back to his feet was a struggle. He smelled smoke, cooked meat, and vegetables. Frank would be with them in the hall for their meal, asking questions. He didn't have time to check.

Using the walls of the cabins for support, Shane stumbled back to the town's western edge and the cabin that had been provided for them. No lights were burning, but a rush of warm air greeted Shane when he opened the door. Frank had built a decent fire before he'd left, and the fireplace was full of softly glowing embers.

Shane stripped, tossing his wet clothes aside and moving to the fire, throwing on a new log before taking the blanket from the bed and wrapping it around him. He waited, warming himself until some sensation returned to his fingers, and then filled a pot with water and placed it over the flames.

The wind continued to howl and rage outside. Shane ignored it, his muscles twitching and shaking as he waited for the warmth to return in the light of a newly stoked fire.

He wasn't sure if he drifted off or if the numbness had affected his senses, but he almost didn't notice the sound of the door opening. If not for the gust of cold air that followed, he might have missed it.

"What happened?" Frank asked, seeing the discarded clothing and Shane's position in front of the fire.

"Took a dip with a ghost," Shane explained.

He had made a cup of tea, something the locals had left in abundance in one cupboard in the small kitchen. It didn't have much taste, but it was hot, and that was all that mattered. He held the cup in his hands as Frank took a chair next to him, removing his gloves and coat and warming his hands.

"You found the so-called spirit of the island, then," Frank said.

"I can't imagine anyone worshipping this thing and thinking it brings a bountiful syrup harvest. Half-eaten, dead-silent, and nimble."

"Eaten," Frank said. "That was how I found Jackson out in the woods."

Shane turned his head to look at the other man.

"Bones cleaned?"

"Very nearly," Frank said. "When I saw you weren't back, I went looking. Found a small crevice stuffed with corpses. Some very old. But Jackson was there."

"Ghost had teeth marks in his bones. Human, for sure."

"Jackson looked the same," Frank said. "Before I left, I was helping to make dinner and asking questions. We made beef stew."

Shane nodded, understanding what Frank was suggesting without saying it. There were no cattle on the island. They could have bought the meat or maybe not. But it wasn't clicking for Shane.

"You spent more time with these people than I did. You think they killed him to eat his body?"

"No," Frank admitted, "but someone took that young man's life. And someone took the meat from his bones."

He had not gotten a cannibal feeling from the people he had met so far. The peaceful, communal aspect didn't seem like it was for show. These people were interested in living a sustainable, organic, old-world lifestyle. They didn't seem like monsters. But they seemed to have fallen in with them.

Shane knew enough about human nature to not discount the fact that they could have killed Jackson. In his experience, few people were above murder given the right circumstances. But killing someone for any reason and eating the corpse were two extremely different things.

There was something more about the island that they were still missing. Ghosts didn't feast on human flesh, but the ghost Shane had seen had been killed the same way that Jackson had, based on what Frank said. If that ghost was a victim and not the spirit of the island these people worshipped, then he and Frank were still mostly in the dark.

"We have a ghost killed the same way as our missing person, and a village full of friendly folks who are lying about it. We're going to need to come at this from a new angle," Shane suggested.

Feeling still had not returned to his feet. He didn't want to get any closer to the fire and risk burning himself accidentally. Frank got up from his seat and began to zip up his coat.

"Tomorrow, then. But for now, I'll get us something to eat. If you trust the stew."

"You made it; you tell me," Shane replied.

Frank headed out and Shane stayed behind, quelling his chattering teeth and twitching muscles with a second cup of tea. He had staved off frostbite, but his core temperature was slow to rise. Outside, the wind howled, and the walls of the cabin creaked. He imagined, if not for the depression into which the village had been built, the storm would have winnowed its way into every crack in the wood.

Despite the ramshackle appearance, the place had a sturdy build that held up well. Whoever had lived on the island before the current residents had been keen on survival. Shane wondered if the cabin builder had been the ghost, the island's spirit demanding sacrifice from its supplicants.

Frank had not closely inspected the bodies, but by his assessment, there were at least a dozen in the woods. He said some were clearly much older than Jackson. It made Shane wonder if there was a routine, or some ritual or scheduled practice behind the deaths.

The islanders were obsessed with natural cycles, so it seemed like something the islanders might do in the spring. Something to bring in good crops. But the timing was certainly off. Maybe it was just incidental because Jackson had discovered something. Or maybe Mallory was a fraud and was killing haphazardly while convincing the rest it was for the greater good.

Shane imagined the older woman not only killing the young man but cutting the meat from his body, chewing on his bones, and eating him raw. It didn't make sense. It didn't fit with anyone else he had met in town, either.

There were other secrets in Maple Grove, then. Someone was hiding a monster. Or they had deceived him incredibly well during his first pass. Shane was a decent judge of character, certainly good enough to identify a cannibal in a village full of hippies, but he felt like a fish out of water now.

Freezing wind blasted through the cabin again, and his thoughts were pulled back into reality as he turned to look at the door. Frank used his shoulder to push it shut and walked across the room to set two bowls on the table.

"Probably cold as hell by now, but I got us dinner." He added some bread from the pack over his shoulder. "Everyone sends their warmest regards and hopes you feel better soon."

"I bet they do," Shane said.

He joined Frank at the table, and they ate their meal. The bread was freshly made, crusty on the outside and soft on the inside. The stew was quite good despite Frank's minor fear that perhaps they were eating human meat. Shane was certain it was beef, and it was tasty and warm and helped him start feeling like his normal self, along with another cup of bland tea.

The sound of snow, wet and thick, splattered against the walls and roof to fill the silences in their conversation. Shane told Frank about the ghost, the graves he had discovered, and the fight that led to him getting dunked in the stream. They traded theories about how much the islanders knew about the small graveyard and the ghost but couldn't agree on anything definitive.

"I think it could be a different ghost." Shane finished his meal. "The one I fought might be another victim. Same as Jackson, only that one came back."

"If the islanders killed him, why isn't he getting revenge?" Frank countered.

"Don't know," Shane said. "He could have killed me, too, but he didn't."

"He almost killed you by freezing you to death."

"That was as much me as him. I didn't know there was a stream until it was too late, and we were in the thick of a fight. I don't know. Something's off about him. He fought well; he could have done more."

"Maybe he just wanted you to leave," Frank said.

"I was thinking that, too. Maybe wanted me away from the graves."

Frank sighed heavily, placed his elbows on the table, and rested his chin on his closed fists.

"I don't know what to do here, Shane. How do I go back to Ted? How do I tell him his boy is dead, and someone did that to him? Left him there like an animal?"

Shane didn't have a good answer. He didn't think there was one. There was the truth, but it was harsh and would comfort no one. And lies would not do, not that Frank would be given to that, even to spare the feelings of a friend.

The door shuddered under the force of the wind. The storm was fully upon them. The people of the village would no doubt be shut in their little cabins, waiting for it to pass.

There was nothing more to be done that night.

CHAPTER 12
SUGAR

The first light of dawn was just barely creeping through the window when Shane opened his eyes. The cabin was warmer than he'd expected. The islanders had provided plenty of warm bedding, and Shane felt much better upon waking than he had when he'd gone to sleep.

Once Frank was awake, the two had a breakfast of dreary tea and hot oatmeal.

"I'm going to track down Alina and see what else she can tell me," Shane said. "She sent us to the woods for a reason."

"I'll see if I can press the others for something new," Frank replied. "Most of these people are unguarded and seem ready to talk. But if they know we found Jackson's body, if that ghost is in contact with Mallory or whoever is responsible, then the day might not go as we plan."

"Didn't think this would be easy, did you?" Shane said.

He was ready to leave first, his clothes crisp and warm after drying on a line near the fire all night. When he opened the door, a drift of snow slipped into the cabin, piled close to two feet high outside.

"Good luck," Frank said. Shane nodded and closed the door behind him.

The village looked buried. There were tracks through the snow where early risers had come and wandered through, but if anyone had a shovel, they hadn't bothered to use it.

Outside the cabin, Shane looked up at the edge of the little bowl that protected the village. Everything was blinding white. He could only imagine how much worse it was up in the field he had struggled through last night, or on the path to the docks.

He made his way through the snow, following the footsteps of two others who had gone before him, and returned to the bright cabin where Alina lived. Most of her decorative touches were hidden beneath a thick, white quilt. There were no tracks to or from her door.

Shane knocked and waited, his breath rising in clouds before his face. The wind was gone, but the cold had set in much harsher than he expected for the time of year.

Some shuffling in the cabin alerted him to the girl's presence before she appeared, her hair messy and her eyes still puffy from sleep.

"Hello?" she said. "You're still here."

"Shouldn't I be?" he replied.

"Mallory told everyone you were leaving today."

"We told her a day or two, but I don't think anyone's going anywhere in this snow. Do you have a moment to talk?" he asked.

Her expression was more than enough of an answer. Her eyes darted around, looking for signs of anyone else on the street outside.

"Not here," she said.

"Then where? I went to the forest. We have some things to discuss."

She shook her head.

"Not in the village. Nothing's a secret here. Meet me at the sugar shack."

Shane raised his eyebrow, and the young woman made a furtive nod to his right.

"Outside the village near the eastern wall by the forest's edge. It's where we process the sap and bottle the syrup."

"The sugar shack," Shane repeated. "When?"

"I'll eat with everyone quickly and then come find you. Give me half an hour."

It was not ideal. Shane didn't want to venture back out into the snow again with that ghost out there.

"What did you want me to find in those woods?" Shane asked.

"Him," she answered. "Please. Meet me at the sugar shack."

She closed the door on him, and Shane grunted softly. It was unclear what she meant by "him". Shane didn't think she was talking about Jackson, but if she had meant the ghost, it was a hell of a thing to send him into. That made it even more perplexing.

Smoke was already rising from the Great Hall as breakfast was prepared. Most of the residents were still indoors, but Shane saw one or two as he left Alina's house and headed back across the small village.

The stares he got on his way past were less friendly than they had been the day before. No one was giving him a hostile look, but Alina's words stuck in his mind. Mallory had told them that he and Frank would be gone. The people looked exasperated when they saw him pass.

He kept his head down and ignored everyone as he trudged across the village to the northeastern side and headed up, out of the bowl, and back into the field. Frank could deal with the locals; he had done well enough so far. Shane was just looking to handle the ghost.

The field of snow outside of the village was nearly blinding. The sky was overcast but not nearly as ominous as it had been the night before. The lack of wind made the walk to where he was going much easier.

He headed east of where he had gone previously, not interested in hitting the forest, and soon enough, he saw a structure in the distance, not far from the edge of the tree line. It was larger than any of the buildings in the village and featured a thick, aluminum smokestack at the top. Nothing was coming from it, and no tracks led to or from the building.

Shane's tracks would give him away if anyone was interested in following. He wondered what the difference was in Alina's mind. Surely, she would have noticed someone listening at her door in the village, but maybe the people were more tech-savvy than they seemed. Maybe Mallory had all the little cabins bugged and was listening to people's secrets. Or maybe the ghost was preying on their vulnerabilities.

There was no lock on the sugar shack door, but Shane needed to clear snow out of the way to pry it open. Inside was as cold as the outside, but there was a sizable boiler and evaporator set up to process the syrup and a small assembly line for bottling and packaging the product.

There was nothing of interest in the shack, nothing out of the ordinary or suspicious. Shane took one of the simple wooden chairs and sat, lighting a cigarette while he waited for Alina. He was halfway through his third one when the door opened, and the young woman appeared.

She frowned and waved her hand through the cloud of smoke.

"You shouldn't do that in here; Mallory will get upset," she said.

"I'll crack a window." He pinched out the cigarette and slipped it back into his pack. "Why did you send me out into that forest?"

The tone in his voice was sharper than it had been, and she picked up on it quickly.

"Did something happen?"

"Yes." He didn't explain further.

"I think that was where Jackson went. They said he left, but he wouldn't have. Without telling me? Not a chance. Did you find something?"

"What did he tell you before he disappeared?" Shane asked.

She was frustrated by his lack of responsiveness, but he sensed that she was on edge as well, eager to talk to someone from outside. When it was clear he wasn't going to answer her question, she continued.

"He wanted to leave. Like, for days. He wanted me to go with him. He said he saw something in town at the altar one night, and it scared him. Something that shouldn't exist."

"What?"

"A monster. A dead thing that wasn't dead. He said it was a man, but he had been cut apart, butchered. But he was walking around. He was real."

"The spirit of the island?" Shane asked.

Alina looked confused, offended even, and shook her head.

"No! Of course not. This island is a good place. It's… pure. The spirit of this place would never be a monster."

Shane sighed and kept his eyes on Alina's.

"I need you to tell me what you mean when you talk about the spirit of this island. I went out into those woods yesterday, and I saw a spirit. Not a metaphor. Not a warm feeling or an idea or a hopeful view of nature. I saw a ghost. The earthly manifestation of a no-longer-living person. And it was the same thing Jackson saw."

Alina's expression was one of utter confusion. Shane could have sworn out loud. For her, the spirit of the island was a metaphor. It was the community spirit or some other hokey thing. She had legitimately thought he would find Jackson in the woods, maybe camping out. It took effort not to relight his cigarette.

"Alina, this island is not a good place," Shane said calmly.

"It is!" she insisted. "At its core, it is. Please, we just need to find Jackson, and—"

"He's dead."

He let the admission hang in the air, cutting her off. He didn't want to be insensitive, but she needed to understand the reality. Maple Grove was not a paradise of sugar shacks and community stews.

She stared, mouth half-open in midsentence, and her eyes were wide and glistening as tears threatened to fall.

"No." She offered a childish shake of her head. "No, you're wrong."

"His body is in the woods. My friend confirmed it was him."

She squeezed her eyes tightly, forcing out the tears as she shook her head harder.

"No. He wanted to leave. He was going to wait for a chance to get a boat, but it got cold. Mallory was being unreasonable, and he was scared, but he's not dead. Maybe your friend thought he was dead, but—"

"Alina," Shane said. "There was no mistake."

"But—"

"He saw the ring; the one Jackson wore. It was still on his finger."

She wouldn't stop shaking her head. She held herself, her arms wrapped tightly, and refused to look at him.

"No. You take me there. You show me because it can't be him. He just wanted to go home."

"It's him. And you don't want to see him."

There was something sharp in his tone, and she picked up on it again. He had meant it to sound neutral. Of course, she wouldn't want to see the man's body. But he knew why, and his tone betrayed the truth of it.

Alina wept. She broke down, crumpling to the floor and sobbing openly. There was something there Shane had seen too often. The acceptance of truth. She had already known Jackson was dead. Part of her knew. But she didn't want to believe it. She wanted to pretend he was there, in the woods, braving cold and hunger in some impossible bid for freedom. She knew better, and now she didn't have to pretend anymore.

"I need to see him," she said softly.

"No, you don't," Shane said. "There's something dangerous in the woods. I've seen it, too. Like a man but cut apart. *Chewed* apart. That's what's here. That's the spirit of this island."

"It can't be," she cried. "That's the same crazy thing Jackson said. It doesn't mean anything!"

Shane crouched in front of the girl and reached out a hand, lifting her face to look her in the eye.

"There is a ghost in that forest. It killed Jackson, and others, and it tried to kill me. You need to believe it if you want to survive."

She shook her head, repeated the word "no" several times, and the sobbing overcame her again. Shane sat back in his chair, let her give in to her grief, and thought of his next move.

A noise at the door startled them. Light flooded the shack as the door opened to reveal Mallory and a man that Shane had not yet met. Mallory's expression was severe as she looked at Shane and Alina as though catching them in an illicit act.

"This is off-limits except during production. You know that, Alina," the woman said, entering the small building.

Alina's demeanor shifted quickly. She wiped her eyes surreptitiously to be unnoticeable as she did so, and immediately, her upset was suppressed. She didn't want to let Mallory know that she had been crying or that anything out of the ordinary had been happening. She stood, sniffled, and nodded.

"Yes. Sorry, Mallory. I just wanted to show Mr. Ryan—"

"Mr. Ryan has greatly overstayed his welcome."

Mallory stared at him, and he pursed his lips before standing.

"I was just asking some questions. Didn't mean to intrude," he told her.

"You did intrude, Mr. Ryan. You trespassed. No one invited you here. Our hospitality was extended to you, and you told us you'd be gone today—"

"We said in a day *or two*," Shane interrupted. "And the weather doesn't look to be cooperating."

"You don't decide, Mr. Ryan. Neither you nor Mr. Benedict decides how long your stay is. And you're right; the weather has made it impossible for you to leave. So, you may return to your cabin with Mr. Benedict, and when it is time to leave, we will let you know."

A second man made himself known at the door; one Shane hadn't noticed. The message was clear enough. Mallory's size was not intimidating, but she was doing her best with her two followers.

Shane glanced at Alina but said nothing. He headed out the door and back into the snow. The two men were silent and looked tough. They followed behind him as he headed back down the path they had walked to reach him.

Frank was waiting when he got back. Two more men waited outside the cabin like guards.

CHAPTER 13

MACHINATIONS

Candles lit the small space, some scented with fresh herbs from the island. The smoky haze was comforting and warm against the cold outside. The place was insulated well enough, but it was not like a modern home on the mainland. It would never be free of drafts or full of modern conveniences, and that was how Mallory wanted it.

Her home was crowded. More than a dozen people crammed into the little space, more than she would usually entertain at one time. She didn't even have enough cups to offer everyone tea, but some had brought their own in anticipation of the problem.

They spoke in hushed tones even though there was no fear of anyone overhearing. The two outsiders were sealed in their cabin on the other side of the village. Edgar and Daniel were watching the door to make sure neither of them left.

"We shouldn't have let them stay," Carmen said, not for the first time.

"We had to," Blaine said. "Turning them away would have raised more suspicion. The police would have returned and been more thorough."

"What does it matter now if they've been to the woods? They already know," someone else added.

"They don't know anything." Mallory drew everyone's attention to her. "From what I heard at the door to the sugar shack, Mr. Benedict found Jackson's body. That's all."

"That's all? They'll call that murder," Carmen said.

"They'll call it nothing," Mallory said. "These men don't know anything. They went to a secluded island in a snowstorm. There is no angle we don't still have control over, and don't forget that."

There was some murmuring from the others, and Carmen lowered her head, shaking it. Small, whispered conversations were to be expected in a group dynamic. In the small space, Mallory heard people whispering about killing. About them being murderers, keeping secrets, and hiding bodies. It was the same thing that had come up again and again over the years.

"What is this I'm hearing?" She raised her voice. "Are you losing faith?"

It was rhetorical, and many of the people avoided eye contact.

"Each one of us has sacrificed for this land. Our blood and sweat are in this soil. This is what we do for the life we want. The life we deserve! Do any of you want to live the way you used to? Back there, back with cars and machines and pollution and hate?"

Scattered answers of "no" filled the room, while others just shook their heads.

"We have found paradise here. The spirit of this land ensures we never want for anything. How many of you could say the same before you came here?"

She looked out at the group, not wanting silence this time. She meant to engage, to force them to see their truth.

"Blaine. You lost your job. Your home. Your wife left, and you lived on the street for how long?"

"Eighteen months," he answered.

"Eighteen months!" she repeated loudly. "In Bangor. In cold winters. In harsh summers. What opportunities did you have to better yourself?"

"None," he said. "None until I found Maple Grove."

Others nodded approval and agreed.

"This place gave you a chance. You give to it; it gives to you. Is it any different for any of you? Carmen? You were on disability, alone, and rotting in a sixth-floor apartment. Was that better?"

"No," the other woman said.

"No!" Mallory shouted. "Nothing we had was better. Nothing could be better. This island lets us be our true selves. We reap what we sow here. We have purpose here, all of us."

"People are dead, Mallory." Carmen's tone was less forceful and less convinced than before.

"They are," Mallory agreed. "And we must never forget them. But are people not dead back in the world we left behind? How many of us would be dead by now?"

There were more nods and mutterings of agreement. Everyone who had made Maple Grove their home had done so because what they left behind was not suitable for them, or nurturing, and it would not have let them thrive or survive. This was more metaphorical for some, but it was literal for many.

Mallory had spent years as part of a tiny sect of a church that her ex-husband brought her into. But with their extreme beliefs and their oppressive nature, they had forced her to become a person she had never imagined herself to be. A person she couldn't even recognize.

When the man she thought she loved had nearly killed her, those people covered it up, assured her that she must have done something wrong, and convinced her that staying and working it out was the right solution. When it happened a second time, they did the same thing again. By the third time, she realized she had to solve problems for herself. And that was what she did.

She fled that place and what she had done, and eventually made her way to the island. With a new name and a new outlook on life, she wanted to leave a controlling world behind and simply live the way nature lets all things live. The island gave that to her.

There was a cost, and she was shocked at first the way anyone would be, but it came to make sense to her. Nature is not without compassion, but it did not suffer fools lightly. Every living thing must earn what it had. Sometimes, it must be taken.

"What about Alina?" Blaine changed the course of the conversation.

Alina had been on the island a far shorter time than the rest of the residents. Mallory wanted the girl to fit in; she already cared for her deeply. But she was becoming a problem. She didn't want to fit in in the way the others did. Already questioning things and working with these outsiders to pick at things no one needed to worry about. If she hadn't invited Jackson, maybe things would have been different. Everything could have been avoided.

"Alina is an issue," Mallory conceded, "but she is a smart girl. She's been here long enough to know the fundamentals of trust and what we expect. If she chooses to violate any of that, it's on her. It's her choice, and if there are consequences, that's on her as well."

"So, what about these men. Frank and his friend?" someone else asked.

"What else can we do?" Blaine added.

Mallory nodded. She wanted others to have the faith that she had. She wanted them to follow the same paths and come to the same conclusions. The only way the island would work was if they were of all the same mind and shared in their beliefs.

It couldn't be her dictating. She would be no different from the people she had escaped from if she espoused violence and told others what to do, told them to hide it. They had to all agree. They had to own it in their souls that what they were doing was right and for the greater good.

It was not an easy battle. A battle against what you had been taught to believe your whole life. Mallory had fought it when she arrived, and the others had done so as well. To accept that sacrifice was the way. Feeding the island's spirit would feed them all. But it worked. They all saw the fruits of their labor. They were all living and thriving the way they had dreamed for so many years when they were imprisoned by poverty, violence, and infirmity. The island was a place to escape from all that. Could any price be too great for such a reward?

"They can't leave," someone said from the back of the room.

Others agreed. If they left, they would cause trouble. They would tell the police and bring more investigators to the island. They would destroy the forest and upset the balance. They would undermine the agreement that existed between the villagers and the spirit of the island. It would be the end of their world.

"So, are we all in agreement as the Elders of Maple Grove? Do we know what must be done?"

More nodding and murmuring, but it grew louder. More passionate.

"Yes."

"Yes!"

Mallory looked at Carmen. The other woman nodded.

"Yes," she said. "We have to protect our home."

The rest of the meeting was spent on planning. Some reassurances where they were needed, because even Mallory had difficulty doing what needed to be done sometimes. That was the personal price they had to pay. None of them should have been calm and accepting of the reality of what needed to be done. It was shocking, and it was meant to be. It proved they still had their humanity that they could feel that way about it.

Frank Benedict and his friend Shane Ryan would have to die. They could not be allowed to leave the island, spread stories of what happened there, and bring an end to the peace that everyone on that island had fought for their entire lives.

When the spirit of the island demanded a sacrifice, it was typically only one. It only needed to be a few times a year. Their gardens would bloom, the trees would give forth the sustenance that kept them prospering, and no one else had to suffer.

There was much suffering in the time before. Many people died. The island spirit could be ruthless and heartless. Mallory suspected that was from the people who had come before. The ones who had built the stone and log cabins. She imagined that they were harsh people. Uncaring and violent. Chopping down the trees, abusing the land, taking from the island, and giving nothing back.

It was Mallory who first spoke to the spirit. It came to her in the shape of a man, ravaged and ruined. She thought it was the perfect metaphor. To appear like the dead. Like something eaten, something consumed. Only she could see it. She thought she'd gone mad, but to save herself at the time, she'd made the deal. Later, she realized that she was not just saving herself, but everyone.

She would give the island a sacrifice, and it would leave the rest of them alone. They prospered greatly from this deal. How was that any worse than what happened back on the mainland? How many people died and got nothing for it? How many people suffered and went ignored? That was not how Mallory ran the island. That was not how the spirit wanted to reward them for their work.

Mallory did not expect any reward from the island for giving two new sacrifices. That was not the way it worked. Nature was not greedy, nor did it offer an abundance to those who already had an abundance. But she hoped it would appreciate their efforts. She hoped it would understand why the new sacrifices were made and would continue to protect them going forward, just as they would protect it.

The sun was setting by the time they had settled on a plan. There were many factors to consider. Not the least of which was worrying about who the two men might have told about the island before they arrived. Everything needed to be meticulous and believable. More people would show up, and they had to expect that and be ready for it. They would be ready this time. This time, they would know what to do and say to make sure there were no more problems.

"This is your last chance," Mallory said to everyone when they were done. "If you have any doubts or reservations, speak now. If not, we're doing what must be done, and we all need each other to be together. The spirit of the island needs us."

She looked around the room. Everyone was steadfast and on board. Everyone met her eyes. There was no resistance.

"Then let's get this done."

CHAPTER 14

GONE

Shane lit another cigarette. Frank assured him he didn't mind Shane smoking in the cabin now that they were not going anywhere. Two men stood outside the door, and no one had said they were prisoners, but they weren't allowed to leave, so that was just a game of semantics.

"Mallory told me she'd clear a path to the docks, and that they would remove us from the island by the morning," Frank said.

"Did you believe her?" Shane asked.

"Until I was brought here and left with guards."

Shane nodded. The fire crackled, but there was no other sound. Even when they whispered, their voices likely carried. He didn't doubt that if someone wanted to hear what they said, it would be easy enough to listen in. No one was being discreet anymore.

"I don't think us being here in the morning is a good idea," Shane said softly.

Frank nodded. They sat at the table. There was nothing else to do, and certainly nowhere to go. They had been in the cabin for two hours already and had compared notes of their encounters with Mallory from earlier in the day. She had been quick and brokered no nonsense in both instances, not wanting to discuss things with the men.

"She must have learned what we saw in the woods and decided the time for putting up a friendly front was over," Frank said.

"Probably," Shane agreed. "I think they were hoping we'd give up when no one had anything to say and leave like the police did. They had to let us in to not look suspicious, but they were on edge the whole time."

"So, their solution…" Frank didn't finish his thought. He didn't need to.

Someone on the island had killed Jackson. Probably the ghost, but someone had mangled his body. Someone had chewed on it, eating the man's flesh. Mallory was obviously part of it, and whether it was her alone or a large group, whatever they were playing at, they couldn't let anyone find out about it.

Shane had to give them credit. Their friendly, simple villager act was very convincing. He doubted Alina knew anything about it, so that meant others were probably in the same boat. But he did not expect an uprising or anyone to stand against Mallory. He expected that the woman would have them killed in the morning. Their bodies would probably be dumped into the same ditch alongside Jackson's. If they were lucky, they wouldn't get eaten, but he couldn't see why it wouldn't happen to him and Frank, if that was the norm on the island.

The door to the cabin opened sometime after the sun had set. Neither Shane nor Frank bothered to get up as Clint entered carrying two bowls of leftover stew and crusts of bread. He looked at the men sheepishly as he approached the table and set down the bowls before turning to walk away without saying a word.

"How are you today, Clint?" Frank asked.

"Not supposed to talk to you anymore." The man did not make eye contact. He stood sideways, facing the wall between the men and the door.

"I understand," Frank said. "Thank you for the food."

"You're welcome." Clint smiled. "I sneaked the bread for you. It's not as good without bread, and—"

"Clint!"

One of the men guarding the door outside yelled at him. Clint shut his mouth and nodded and then turned away from Frank and Shane, heading out of the cabin. The door was pulled closed behind him, and the two men were left alone once more.

"Not everyone on this island is part of this," Frank said.

"I know." Shane lifted the bowl of food to his nose and smelled it. Would the islanders be above poison? He didn't think so.

Frank watched him, spoon in hand. He stopped himself from digging in.

"Is it safe?"

"Can't tell. Bread probably is if it was a gift from Clint."

Despite being the only person to brandish a weapon against them, Shane was fairly certain Clint was out of the loop like Alina. But he didn't believe that people like Clint or Alina had the power to help them. If anything, they were also at risk.

They ate bread and drank tea and chatted softly about the island, the ghost, and their plans without being specific. Shane didn't think anyone on the island was a fighter. He was confident he could have taken on the two men at the door on his own if he needed to. No one had searched his belongings since he had been there to realize he had brought a gun with him if it came to that.

The bigger problem was the island. Shane would be surprised if Mallory did not have control of the radios. Getting a message to Mo back on the mainland was their only option short of commandeering one of the boats docked there. And that might not be an option, either.

Residents aside, the island spirit was a killer. He was strong and smart, and he had let Shane live once. Maybe he wouldn't make that mistake again.

Frank took a bite of the stew, and Shane raised an eyebrow.

"Tastes fine," he said.

"Forgive me if I wait to see how you feel in an hour."

"Harsh. But fair, I suppose. I don't think these people want to poison us. They just want us gone."

"So they can keep killing people."

Frank shook his head.

"It's not everyone, Shane. I know it isn't."

Shane knew Frank was right, but he also didn't think it mattered. If you were held prisoner by ten people and three of them wanted you dead, there was a good chance you would be dead in the morning. That was the position they were in.

He was about to continue the conversation when a noise drew his attention to the rear of the cabin near the small bathroom. The men fell silent, and Shane cocked his head, listening more closely. The noise came again, a distinct but very subtle tapping of something against glass.

Shane nodded to Frank, and the other man continued talking, carrying on an imaginary conversation to distract anyone who might be listening. Shane approached the small window and peered out, surprised to see a dark form on the other side, hands pressed to the glass and staring in at them.

"Alina?" Shane pressed close to the wall so she could hear him.

"Where is Jackson?" Her voice was barely audible.

"Alina, you don't—"

"I'm going to find him. Are you going to help me or not?"

She hissed the words, and Shane shook his head.

"It's not safe," he insisted.

"It doesn't matter. I need to see him. Please, help me."

"You will die if you go out there."

There was no response from the girl, and Shane wasn't sure she had heard him. He waited a beat and then looked out the window again, but she was gone.

Frank was still talking to himself at the table when Shane returned. He leaned close and nodded back the way he had come.

"Alina. She's gone to the woods to find Jackson," he said.

Frank grimaced. He knew better than Shane what waited for her out there. They couldn't let her go, but what were their choices? Stuck in the cabin as they were, if she had already left, they would need to find a way past their guards.

Shane and Frank looked one another in the eye. Frank had not stopped talking. He was saying mundane things about the stew, prattling on in a droning voice that was sure to bore anyone listening outside. Shane occasionally chimed in with a word of affirmation or a grunt, but every so often, he lowered his voice so that only Frank could hear.

"We have to go after her," he said.

"Agreed," Frank said.

Despite his better instincts, Shane felt responsible for the girl. She had held out hope that Jackson was still around, despite the time that had passed, the weather, and everything that was working against him. She might have been a little naïve, or maybe a lot naïve, but Shane was the one who brought reality down on her. Shane was the one who shattered her world. It was the right thing to do, but he had set into motion the path she was now on.

"How do you want to play this?" Frank asked softly.

"Give it a few minutes. Quiet down. Let them get bored."

Frank nodded. The men guarding them were not skilled or adept at what they were doing in any way. Shane and Frank would be able to leave without them having any idea.

Shane went to the back window first. He took the pillow from the bed, pressed it against the glass, and used his elbow to break through the pane, making as little noise as possible.

He cleared the glass out as quickly as he could and then gave Frank the all-clear after sticking his head out to see behind the cabin. No guards were back there, only snow and some scattered trees. He saw Alina's footprints leading away from them and up the bowl out into the fields beyond.

Frank brought their winter gear, passed it to Shane, and then climbed out the window with him. There was no way to know how long they had before someone from the village opened the door to check on them, but neither man was overly concerned.

Skirting behind the few remaining cabins before they left the village, they followed Alina's footprints and headed across the field of snow toward the forest. The girl's head start was not long, but the ghost would not need much time to finish her off if it caught her.

It was easy enough to track her as far as the edge of the forest, but beyond the tree line was another matter. The snow became spotty, and there were intermittent chunks of dead leaves and mud that poked through.

There were places where it seemed like she had weaved back and forth, unsure where to go. Without the light to guide them, it was harder to follow a direct path, but they wound up at the ring of graves in the center of the small clearing.

"Nothing there," Frank said, noticing the undisturbed snow in the center of the stones. Shane backtracked slightly and found something that looked like a trail again, following it to the east away from the graves and closer to where Frank had found the bodies.

Frank took the lead, directing them away from the circle of stones and heading toward what he thought was the right direction. There were no longer any signs of Alina in the woods, and Shane doubted she had followed back in her footprints. Something had taken her, and it had done so without leaving tracks.

"Something's wrong." Frank slowed his pace. "I recognize this area, but you could smell them before."

"Could all be frozen," Shane said. The other man shook his head.

"Should have been frozen before. The smell was strong. Death and rot. Not even a hint of it now."

He led them a little deeper into the woods and stopped next to a leaning maple tree that hung over a split in the earth. Shane stared into the crevice and saw nothing but mud, dried leaves, and a smattering of snow.

"They were all here." Frank crouched.

He had told Shane a significant number of corpses were in the pit. For them to all be gone now was not the work of the islanders.

"I think we have an answer." Shane nodded beyond the ravine.

Several yards away, crouched between a pair of thick tree trunks, the ghost that Shane had fought with watched the men. Frank saw him now for the first time, and the ghost watched them with what looked like disinterest on what was left of his face.

"Watch yourself. He's a lot faster than he looks." Shane prepared to meet the ghost if it came at them.

Almost as though the spirit had heard, he rose and turned away from the two men. A moment later, he was gone.

Shane arrived where the ghost had been a step ahead of Frank. The dead man had obviously left no tracks, but there was also no sign that he had taken Alina. No footprints, no blood splatters, and no sign of a struggle. Shane didn't know what to make of it or of the ghost's unpredictable nature.

They followed in the direction the ghost had gone, brief though his appearance was. There was still no sign of Alina as they went, and soon, they reached the east coast of the island, the trees dwindling away until they were at a stony cliff that descended in a sheer drop to the ocean on the other side. Gray water crashed against the stone, and the air was cold and salty.

There was no sign of the girl or the ghost.

CHAPTER 15
In Flames

Little was said as Frank and Shane continued back through the forest. The only place they picked up Alina's trail was where they had initially left it. It ended by the time she reached the circle of graves. They ventured north and west of the circle and found nothing in either direction. The girl was gone. Alive or dead, there was no way to know.

It was getting late. It wouldn't be long before the villagers noticed they were gone, if they hadn't noticed already. They couldn't afford to spend much more time out in the forest. The cold crept in, the insidious kind that seeped through boots and clothes and made its way into one's bones. Alina was as much at risk as the men if not more, but they could do nothing else for her.

They broke for the village, heading south again. Frank stopped them as they passed tapped trees and crunched through dead leaves and wet snow, catching sight of the ghost waiting for them as though he had known what path they would follow.

"Why does he do that?" Frank asked. "Why does he just watch us?"

"You can ask him if you like," Shane replied.

Shane had mostly given up on questioning the whims of ghosts. Some would just never be understood. A ghost like this had to have suffered mentally and physically. Shane wondered how much of the man he once was existed in the half-eaten, mutilated frame. How much had been torn away by the teeth that took his life?

"Hello!" Frank took Shane's words to heart.

Shane almost laughed but instead just shook his head, holding back as the other man took a step toward the spirit with his hand raised in a friendly wave.

"I was hoping we could talk for a moment. Figure out if there's something we can do to help you, maybe. We're looking for the girl who came out here. If you know where she is, if she's still alive, we'd like to take her back home before anything happens."

To Shane's surprise, the ghost watched Frank, head slightly cocked and listening to the man. He was crouched in the snow, half-obscured by the trunk of a maple tree, his bloody, almost chewed-away arms resting across equally bony knees. It seemed like at least for a moment, the ghost might answer.

Frank continued toward the spirit and Shane, trailing behind, kept his eye on the ghost. Shane thought Frank was being too bold, but he didn't say anything. It wasn't his place to tell Frank how to handle ghosts; the man knew what he was doing. But that didn't mean it was the right approach.

"If you tell me what you want, what you need from us or the villagers, I'm sure we can find a way to ensure everyone is satisfied."

Frank was within a few yards of the ghost. The spirit shifted his weight, leaning slightly to one side, and then without a word, he bounded forward like a dog given a command.

The ghost was on Frank before Shane even moved. He threw the older man to the ground, pushing him into the snow as grisly, skeleton hands then lifted him by the front of his jacket and hurled him at Shane to cut off a counterattack.

Frank collided with Shane, and both men fell to the ground. Shane rolled Frank roughly to the side, unconcerned about his friend's condition, and quickly got to his feet to meet the ghost head-on. Instead of a fight, the ghost had already vanished again.

Shane cursed. He didn't understand the game the ghost was playing. Why would it be aggressive and then pull away? It was toying with them, but it made no sense. Why keep letting them go if it was so willing to tear villagers to shreds?

"Where is he?" Frank joined Shane a moment later.

"Good question. Let's not wait to find out."

They left the forest, trudging across the snowfield and back toward the village. Shane saw nothing following them. From his vantage, there was no sign that Alina had returned, nor had anyone left to find them or her, but the night hid any trails that might have strayed too far east.

The guards were still stationed outside of the cabin when they returned. Frank and Shane crept around to the window, sneaking back in the way they had left as quietly as they could. The broken window had allowed the cold to creep in and fight with the fire, but it was a small price to pay. Shane filled in the window with one of the blankets as best he could, sealing out the cold air while Frank added another log to stoke the flames.

"Bowls are gone." Frank stood at the table. Their leftovers had been cleared. Someone had been in the cabin while they were gone and was aware that they were missing. "Why were they still guarding the door?"

His answer came in the form of hammering. Shane quickly returned to the window at the back of the cabin. A plank of wood had been pressed over it on the outside. It was being hammered to the wall on both sides, two men working quickly and forcefully, pounding nails into the panel to secure it and seal them in.

"Check the door," Shane said.

Frank tried the handle to the door, but it wouldn't budge. He banged his fist against it, rattling the door and its frame.

"A little overdramatic guys, don't you think?" he said.

He heard people talking outside, but the voices were muffled. There was more hammering, at the door, and a nail pierced the space between two timbers.

"Same thing over here," Frank said.

Wisps of smoke filtered through the cracks around the door. Shane swore as Frank backed away. It only took moments for the first orange flickers of flame to appear. The islanders had lit the cabin on fire. They were going to burn Shane and Frank alive.

Frank began to yell, pounding on the door as he tied his scarf over his face to prevent smoke inhalation. Shane tried to clear the panel from the back window, but the men outside continued to hammer the plank of wood. It was heavy and thick, and they had secured it quickly but firmly. Even slamming his shoulder into it didn't budge the wood.

Smoke rose to the ceiling of the cabin in thick, gray tendrils. Frank had switched from knocking on the door to kicking it, to get anyone outside to talk to him. He heard muted chatter from several villagers out there, but no one replied.

Shane gave up on escaping through the window and began to search the cabin, running his hands along the walls. He felt the texture of the wood, and the gaps between the timbers, and pushed wherever he felt anything unusual or out of place.

"Here," he said to Frank after a moment. "Grab a log."

Frank grabbed one of the larger, thicker logs next to the fireplace and Shane did the same. He led him to a place in the wall near the bed. Although the cabin was well-made, there was a larger gap between the timbers there. It had been packed and insulated, but it looked to Shane like the weakest point in the construction.

Shane slammed the end of the log against the wall like a hammer and pulled back. Frank did the same, and the two fell into a rhythm. The timbers shook, and mud and grit fell from the cracks in the wall. Smoke covered the ceiling, and flames had taken hold of the inside of the door.

People were still talking outside. Some were yelling, but the voices were muffled. Shane didn't care what they said; they just needed to get away from the structure before it was too late.

Again and again, Shane and Frank slammed the logs into the wall.

Back and forth, both swinging as hard as they could, hammering into the structure to loosen just one of the logs.

The smoke grew thicker, and Shane pulled his shirt over his face to prevent as much smoke inhalation as he could. Neither he nor Frank said anything, though they shared glances now and then, as the door was consumed by fire and the heat of the cabin increased.

Soon enough, the surrounding walls were burning. The cabin was old, and the wood was very dry. It would not hold up long.

"Shane." Frank stopped for a moment and breathed heavily behind his scarf, which soon led to a bout of coughing.

"Keep going," Shane replied.

He slammed the chunk of wood as hard as he could, with the gloves on his hands absorbing some of the blow. More dust and dirt fell free. A second hit took up the slack for Frank as the other man caught his breath.

The spot Shane had originally felt, the little gap between timbers, tumbled free to expose a hole to the outside. Shane hit the spot again and heard a creak as the wood finally shifted.

The two men looked at each other and, still coughing, Frank took up his swings again. They focused on the same small area, the same narrow piece of wood, and a crack quickly became a split.

Shane slammed his heel into the wall and forced out the timber. Another followed quickly, and the surrounding logs buckled. Frank tossed aside the firewood he had been using, and they worked the wall with their feet until the rear corner of the cabin collapsed, timbers falling from up near the ceiling and almost hitting them in the process.

Two of the villagers came at them as Shane climbed over the pile of rubble he had created out into the snow, slinging his bag over his shoulder. He didn't look to see who it was before taking a swing, knocking out the first man with a punch directly to the face.

The fire spread through the cabin behind them, and the second villager backed off, turning and running quickly as Shane and Frank left them behind, following their own tracks back up the side of the bowl and out of the village.

A gunshot rang out behind them, wide and to the left. Someone was firing a rifle, but Shane didn't look to see who it was or whether they were able to improve their aim. He scrambled through the snow to the sounds of men shouting. A second gunshot flew just as wide in the other direction. He almost wanted to thank them for being such poor shots but instead made a beeline for the woods with Frank at his side.

Three men from the village pursued them, but Shane and Frank had put a good distance between them by the time their pursuers reached the edge of the snow-covered bowl that protected their little village. Another gunshot rang out, and it was so far off the mark that Shane couldn't tell where it went. In the poor light, and with little skill, none of the villagers seemed to have any idea what to do with a firearm.

The hospitality of Maple Grove Island was over. Shane and Frank would have to survive in the forest until they got back to the boats or a radio.

CHAPTER 16
THE EATER

The men of the village barely pursued Shane and Frank. They fired shots and shouted into the night but had no resolve to continue. Either from fear of what might happen if they followed or confidence that the cold and the ghost would take care of them, the chase ended quickly.

"East," Shane said when it was clear no one was behind them. There was no reason to enter the forest, no reason to give the ghost another chance to get them between the trees. Not that anything was stopping it from coming at them in the open fields, but at least they would see it more easily if that was the case.

Instead, Shane directed them toward the sugar shack. It was not ideal, and the locals would surely look there if they pursued the men during the light of day, but it would get them through the night. Shane was confident that no one would burn it down on them when it seemed to be the source of the island's income. If anyone confronted them there in person, he welcomed the chance to let them try.

"There's an evaporator," Shane pointed out once they entered the structure. "Good-sized boiler; probably gets really warm in here. We should be fine for the night."

"Until they come looking for us." Frank was already gathering wood from a pile to get the fire lit.

"I imagine we'll have a visitor from the woods before any of them work up the nerve to confront us after that stunt," Shane replied.

Frank shook his head, setting some kindling alight in the large cast-iron furnace beneath the evaporator.

"I'm stunned. I didn't expect that. I thought I was connecting with these people."

"I know," Shane said.

"Some of them told me about their children. Their grandchildren! They're not monsters."

Shane chuckled.

"They just tried to burn you alive," Shane reminded him.

"They did." Frank was disheartened. Maybe even hurt. Frank was a good man, but he let his emotions play too close to the surface in situations that needed detachment.

By the time the fire was lit, and the shack was warming up, both men had settled down across from it with a view of the windows and the door should anyone enter.

"Does the worst in people ever drag you down?" Frank asked.

"Used to it now," Shane replied.

They sat across from one another. The heat was slow to fill the large space. It was not meant to be used as a heater, just a way to boil sap, but they had overfilled the chamber and left the door open. It would keep them alive.

"Do you want to be used to it? I like to imagine a time, a place, some world where people are inherently good all the time. Where darkness is a perverse and unusual thing to be shunned."

"Do you?" Half a smile curled Shane's lip.

"I'm not a child," Frank said. "I don't mean it like that. Some fantasyland where we all hold hands. God, I don't even want that. But was basic decency ever the norm, do you think? Shouldn't it be? Society must have started that way. People putting aside mistrust to work together to build something bigger and better."

"Sure," Shane said. "Problem is when people a hundred generations later have everything and take that for granted. They never needed to collaborate to make things work. Now they want to hoard it for themselves and look at you like an outsider, not a comrade."

"Isn't this place the former, though? They came here to work together. To make something better."

"And then?" Shane said.

Frank sighed loudly.

"Then they decided to sacrifice people to a monster. I'm just thinking out loud. This has been a hell of a job. I never expected to find that boy alive. I hoped I would, but I knew it was unlikely. But these people? I just didn't expect this."

"People will surprise you," Shane agreed. "Just not always the way you want."

"Is it as hard as it seems? Dealing with not just the dead but those who crave it? I avoid that when I can, but it seems like you're always knee-deep."

"I don't think I'm cut out for helping people like you do." Shane shrugged. "Maybe that's for the best. You work out solutions I can't. I work out ones you can't."

"And here we both are, trapped in a maple syrup processing shack on an island from which we can't escape while a village of strangers tries to kill us."

"Don't forget the ghost," Shane said. "And our mystery cannibal."

"Of course," Frank agreed. "And the cannibal."

The night wore on, but the shack grew warm, and they were at least comfortable. The hour was late, well past midnight, when the silence outside was shattered by a man's screams.

Shane awoke with a start. He hadn't realized he'd fallen asleep. The exertion of searching the island, struggling through the snow, and dealing with the locals had exhausted him more than he realized. But he was awake and listening intently as cries from the outside came through the walls.

He was up faster than Frank, peering out the window into the darkness for signs of the locals approaching. The night sky offered not even starlight, and if there were men in the fields, they carried no lights.

The scream came again, and Shane focused on it. An ill-defined shape in the darkness, highlighted by the white snow background. It was being dragged across the field.

"We need to help—" Frank began to say.

As if in answer, the man's screams cut off with a wet gurgle. Shane watched the shadowy shape of the ghost tear at the dead man's neck. The details were lost to the darkness, but it didn't take much imagination to figure out what was happening. Moments later, the ghost resumed dragging the body, now silently, until both had vanished into the maple forest.

Shane left the window, and Frank took his place. He stared out as though he might see something that Shane missed, or if somehow by watching, the man would come back to life, and they would be able to help him. By the time he sat down again, Shane was warm enough to unzip his coat and lean against the wall.

"I wanted to help these people," Frank said. "I wanted to help Jackson, and I thought maybe I could do some good here with the others. They're idealistic and naïve, but I don't think the world should punish you for that. We need to leave this place. But we can't leave them with that ghost."

"I know," Shane replied. How many times had he told Frank that now? It was more like Frank was convincing himself of something. Maybe that goodness he was talking about. Shane's concerns were elsewhere.

He was not a fan of being backed into a corner. The rational part of his mind said they needed to track down a boat or a radio. It would have been so simple anywhere else in the world. But even on that damn island, it would eventually happen. Or that's how it should have worked. But if they left, they were condemning everyone else to die. Alina, if she was still alive, Clint, and whoever else had gotten caught up in their foolish ideals.

"These people are giving up their own to a ghost. Someone here is eating people. I'll destroy the spirit, but the villagers are on their own."

"They're not all—"

"Yeah, I get it." Shane interrupted Frank. "But enough of them are. Like I said, I'm all in for destroying that ghost and ending the living gravy train. If you want to talk to the people who just tried to light us on fire, that's on you."

"Fair enough." Frank sighed. "But you need to have some compassion. A lot of these people have been lied to. It has to be Mallory or at least her inner circle."

"Yeah, Grandma's got a hunger for the flesh of man and has decided it's the key to ensuring delicious pancakes." Shane gestured at the syrup bottles on the far wall.

They stayed up talking for a short while longer. Once Shane was satisfied that no one from the village would venture out in the dark, doubtlessly more afraid of the ghost than they were of the men hidden in the sugar shack, they got some rest.

Shane awoke as the sky outside was beginning to lighten. The cloud cover was not going away, but the pale, gray light encroached on the land. If they didn't leave soon, Mallory and her people would come for them.

They would have to abandon the shack and head to the forest. They could cross the island that way, reach the far shore out of sight, and gain access to a boat before anyone knew what they were doing.

They left with few words exchanged. Shane took the lead and went around the back of the shack so that if anyone showed up, they would not immediately see which direction the men had gone. He went wide around the structure, north, and then west into the confines of the forest.

The ghost had not been shy with Shane so far. He knew they were walking into a potentially dangerous situation, but he was not convinced they would be ambushed. The spirit was open, taunting really, and would show itself before an attack.

"If we see the ghost, we destroy it, here and now," Shane said as they marched between the trees. "Otherwise, we find the coast and secure a boat. If need be, you can take one, and I'll finish things and then join you."

"I'm not leaving you alone," Frank said.

Shane glared at him.

"You work alone all the time; I understand that. This is my fight, too. I'm the one who brought us here. I won't leave this behind just to secure a way out."

Shane grunted. Frank was right. He had a place in all of this, and it was mildly insulting for Shane to suggest that he should secure their escape and wait for Shane to finish the work. He wasn't a random person helping Shane out. But, as Frank pointed out, Shane was used to working alone. It was easier when he didn't have to worry about what someone else was doing.

As much as he appreciated the company and the insight, Frank could not fight. Ventura could not fight. Jacinta had not been able to fight. Aside from Thomas Coulson, few people he'd worked with could hold their own. The nature of the job was a solitary one. Partners and friends all eventually became liabilities.

They cut across the woods slowly and carefully, watching for movement. Alina was still unaccounted for. The ghost would be out there somewhere, probably already watching them. And they still had the villagers to worry about, if they were willing to brave the woods.

"There," Frank said after they had been walking for a half-hour.

Blood-stained snow greeted them, the red splatters growing darker and more abundant the longer they followed them through the trees. Shane rounded a pair of maples growing almost on top of each other and stopped on the far side, looking down at the body of a man.

He vaguely recognized him, one of the villagers, probably the man who had been dragged into the woods the night before. The skin was removed from his face and most of his chest and arms. Someone had even cracked the ribs and pulled out his organs.

"Bites." Frank pointed at the humerus.

There was a perfect imprint of irregular teeth. One of the front ones was crooked and sat at a slight angle to the one next to it. Most of the bites were light and didn't leave imprints, just scrapes, but a few managed to sink in from more force and aggression.

"Looks unfinished," Shane said.

The lower half of the man's body had not been touched. His pants were soaked in blood, but the flesh had not been exposed. The ghost Shane had seen had been nearly stripped from head to toe, and Frank had mentioned much the same about Jackson's body. It looked like someone had interrupted the ghost before he finished his work.

"The ghost did this." Frank sounded almost surprised.

Shane nodded. It had been hard to see in the night, but there was no way villagers had taken the body away, and the man was most definitely alive, at least for a while. That meant that the cannibal they were looking for was the ghost.

"Explains a bit."

"How do you mean?" Frank asked.

"Erratic behavior," Shane said. "Why he let me go, and why he didn't attack us yesterday. If this is the way that he died, he likely lost his mind. We can't predict what he'll do next. He eats flesh to stay alive when there's no reason for it. He might not even understand that he's dead."

It put a new spin on things, one Shane had not expected. Mallory, and those in league with her, were feeding people to the ghost. It was not able to devour them. It could not swallow the meat or digest it, but it could still tear the flesh and kill its victims in the most horrible way.

"Let's keep moving," Shane said.

They could offer the dead man nothing.

CHAPTER 17

CORNERED

Shane stood still. Next to him, Frank looked to the northeast, held his breath, and scanned the horizon. They had both heard the sound, a distant shout coming from deeper in the woods, deeper than Shane had even gone before, back toward the coast.

"Sounded like a man, don't you think?" Frank asked.

Shane shook his head, waiting to hear more. It had been a quick sound like a cry of surprise. It was too quick and too far off to definitively say it had been a man. They were thinking the same thing: It could have been Alina. She could have been out there, somehow having survived the ghost and the cold.

He started moving and Frank stayed behind a moment longer, about to say something but thinking better of it and simply following the other man. They were not quite backtracking, but they were heading east again when the boats were to the west. After what had happened with the man the night before, it would be madness for any villager to willingly enter those woods. Unless Mallory kept a tight rein on all information and no one was aware of what happened, which could have also been the case.

Shane and Frank moved in the general direction of the sound, crossing the stream that Shane had nearly drowned in the day before, and heading into thicker woods. It only took a few minutes of travel before they picked up more sounds. More than one this time, multiple shouts from several people. Not the ghost, then; someone else.

They moved quickly and quietly, staying behind the trees and being as stealthy as they could. The forest thinned out as they approached the eastern wall and the rocky, jagged cliffs that led to the ocean far below.

No one was there. Shane looked up and down the edge of the cliff. Neither villager nor ghost stood among the stones or scant trees.

"There." Frank pointed to the ground.

In the snow, tracks led to the rocks, to the edge of the cliff, and then ventured into the stone to a path unseen. The men got closer and looked down. A trail, narrow and precarious, led through the rocks and down the side of the cliff toward the sea. From their vantage point, it was impossible to see where it went, but it was wide enough for a man to walk safely.

Raised voices rose up the cliffside, muffled by the white noise of crashing waves below. A landing was down there somewhere, a smaller cliff or a cave or something. It was impossible to see how many people, but Shane made out at least three voices.

Shane took the lead after one more look around. No other people were around. The ghost was nowhere to be seen, either.

It was a dangerous path, and the risk of falling was high, never mind the risk of a confrontation that could have ended with someone being thrown off. Shane hoped having the high ground and the element of surprise would give them the edge if it came to that.

"You're coming back one way or another," a man said angrily.

Shane slowed, indicating for Frank to do the same. The path led down at a soft incline that widened ahead but also curved around a stony jut that obscured what lay on the other side.

The ocean was mostly gray below, and white caps rolled toward the rocks maybe thirty yards beneath the stone landing. Nothing was visible on the horizon. Maple Grove might as well have been alone in the universe.

Shane heard a woman's voice, more muffled than the one that had spoken earlier. He couldn't make out the words, but the emotion was clear. She was afraid, pleading. Alina. Somehow, she had survived, but the other villagers were after her now.

"… Jackson's dead! Mallory is lying to us. She lied to you!" Shane heard Alina say as he approached the curve in the stone path.

He looked back at Frank, and the other man nodded his readiness. Shane turned the corner, walking out onto a flat surface before the wide mouth of a cave that extended some ten yards into the cliff face.

The platform was so flat that it looked almost man-made. The cave was plain and empty save for a fire burning next to a blanket and a pack of supplies. Alina stood before it while three men from the village faced her down.

One man held a rifle, and Shane recognized him as one of the men who was always with Mallory. Blaine, he thought his name was. The other two were familiar, but he didn't remember their names.

"Blaine!" one of the men shouted, seeing Shane come around the corner.

Blaine turned quickly, raising the rifle and backing up a step so his gun was pointed at Shane, and he was standing between his men and Alina.

"Hold it," Blaine said.

Shane raised his hands lazily but took another two steps forward to keep himself from the cliff's edge. Frank rounded the corner as well, hands already raised, and Blaine shifted the rifle to aim at him and then back at Shane.

"Both of you need to stop, or you're dead men," he warned.

"No one needs to die today," Frank said. "Blaine, come on. I came here to look for a lost kid whose dad misses him, and this is what you're doing? You'd kill me for that?"

"Enough of the nice guy act, Frank. We know you've been doing more than just looking for Jackson. You're ruining everything we have here. You're going to take everything we have here."

"How?" There was genuine confusion in Frank's voice.

Shane stayed where he was, watching Blaine and the other two men. One of the others had a rifle, a Winchester Model 100. It was older than any of the men there, and the stock had a noticeable crack in it. Blaine was sporting a Ruger No. 1 that was newer than the Winchester, but barely.

The man with the Winchester had it aimed at the ground. He was holding it in one hand, above the trigger guard more like a club than a gun. Blaine, at least, had a grip on the weapon, but his finger was on the trigger, not the guard. Shane suspected that was more unfamiliarity with handling a weapon than it was intent to shoot. Just as dangerous. Moreso, really. The man was careless and untrained. A gust of wind could spook him, and he'd fire off a round.

"This isn't going to be a discussion," Blaine said.

"Stop it!" Alina stepped closer to the armed man. "Jesus, Blaine. Are you going to kill them? Are you a murderer now?"

"Alina." Blaine's jaw tightened. "You should leave. Now."

"No," she said. "I'm not going back there. You're going to have to kill me, too."

"Alina, come on," the unarmed man said.

"No!" she shouted. "You are not listening to me. Someone killed Jackson. I saw him! I saw what happened to him, and it's not good. It is not for us, the island, or the trees. It was... it was horrible."

"Alina, shut your mouth." Blaine kept the gun on Frank. "You two can turn the hell around."

"No," Shane said simply.

Blaine furrowed his brow in confusion and pointed the gun at Shane, taking a step forward.

"Do you think this is a joke, tough guy? I have the gun, and you will do what I say. You and your friend go to the ledge and face the ocean."

"No," Shane lowered his hands and sighed with a shake of his head before turning to Alina. "How did you survive the night?"

"I'm the one with the gun here!" Blaine lifted the barrel into the air and fired a round into the sky that made Alina and the men with him flinch. Shane sighed again.

"Turn around." Blaine leveled the gun at Shane once more.

"Or?"

"What?" Blaine snapped the question out, confusion mixing with rage. Shane heard Frank make a soft warning sound, but he ignored it.

"Or what? You going to kill me right here? Not going to take me to Mallory and get some orders?"

Shane saw the rage build in Blaine's eyes. His finger tensed and Shane stayed calm, pushing the gamble as far as he dared.

"Blaine," Winchester guy said. "We have to take him to Mallory. She wants all of them."

"Yeah," Blaine said sourly.

"Come on, man. This is a good thing. We got all three of them. This is what we needed to do."

Shane could see Blaine debating what to do. He was the island tough guy; that was easy enough to see. He was Mallory's muscle, as much as anyone could be considered that. Maybe the role had gone to his head. He looked to Shane like the kind of guy who bought one drink at a bar and spent three hours eating free pretzels. He had a greasy, burnout quality to him, but it seemed that the island had given him some degree of responsibility. Mallory had entrusted him as an enforcer. He liked being a bully. He liked being a big man.

"Get back up," Blaine said finally, gesturing to the path. "You too, Alina. We're all going back to the village."

"I am not—"

Blaine turned on her and rushed forward. Shane tensed but didn't move as Blaine pressed the barrel of the weapon right into the girl's face, digging into her cheek, and forcing her to look away from him.

Alina gasped, her body going rigid as her eyes locked on Shane with her face forced toward him. Shane gave her a simple nod.

"Fine." Her voice was strained. "Let me get my stuff, at least."

"Make it fast," Blaine ordered.

The girl grabbed her bag and kicked the logs fueling her fire. Blaine kept the gun on her and followed her as she left the cave and then passed Shane and Frank toward the path that ran up the side of the cliff.

"Frank." Blaine pointed the gun at him. "You go next. Mouthy, you go at the back so if I need to blow someone's brains out, it's you."

Frank followed Alina up the path and Shane followed him. The other two men fell in line behind Blaine. Without turning his head, Shane heard Blaine just a couple of steps behind him. It would have been easy enough to turn, grab the barrel of the Ruger, and throw the man off the cliff. He probably could have tossed his two friends after him, as well.

Instead, he just followed Frank. There was more to learn about the relationship between the villagers and the ghost, and Frank wasn't ready to sacrifice that just yet. Blaine was part of the inner circle, the Elders. He might have had valuable information. Even if it meant Shane would have to beat it out of him later.

Once they were back up top, Alina stopped not far from the edge of the cliff, waiting for Shane and the others to catch up. Blaine had no interest in stopping. He pushed the barrel against Shane's back and forced him to keep moving, encouraging the others to do the same.

"Back home," Blaine said. "Storm's coming, no need to waste time."

Shane looked at the sky. Dark clouds rolled in from the south, black and ominous. A southern storm should not have been so bad, but the storms on the island were not typical. Shane didn't think anything was natural about the clouds that moved in.

Blaine marched them into the woods while Shane searched the darkening forest for signs of the ghost. It was still so early in the morning, but the clouds stole the sunlight, and gusts of freezing wind cut through the maples.

"This looks bad, Blaine," Winchester guy said.

"Just keep walking; we'll be there in just a few minutes," Blaine replied.

Snow began falling, whipped by the frenzied winds. Shane saw nothing stalking the woods, but the ominous darkness grew like a living thing. The approaching storm seemed to come not just from above but below. The ghost had to be involved, an illusion of some kind, drawing in the weather. But the cold was real enough. Deadly enough.

And it was coming on fast.

CHAPTER 18

FROZEN

The black clouds seemed to descend from the sky, hanging low over the island. Sleet whipped through the trees in fat, loose gobs. With the wind behind it, the freezing effect was even more noticeable. They were walking into it, facing the onslaught, so any exposed flesh was at risk of being pelted and nearly frozen the moment it hit.

Shane expected to see the ghost approach at any moment, but there was no movement in the trees. It was too hard to predict what it would do. None of its actions made sense to Shane. Why would it kill a person one moment, try to eat them, and then avoid contact the next?

Even if it had been driven mad by its injuries, there should have been some consistency in that madness. It should have been attacking or stalking. But it seemed wholly rational when Shane fought it. It didn't speak, but its movements were measured. It acted as if it knew what it was doing.

Alina was slowing at the head of the group, an arm raised in front of her face to shield herself from the wet snow. Frank offered her his scarf, and Blaine shouted at them again.

"Keep moving!"

Alina muttered something as she stopped, turning to face the others, the wind whipping at the scarf around her face.

"You don't have to do this, Blaine. We need to work together to get away from this place. We—"

"Alina, I swear to God." Blaine raised the gun again.

"Forget it," Shane told her, his back still to the other man. "He's not the kind of man who can listen or think for himself. He likes doing what he's told."

"Buddy, your mouth is going to get you dead before you know it." Blaine turned the gun and slammed the butt between Shane's shoulder blades. With the padding of his winter jacket on, he barely even felt the blow. Blaine was more bluster than the storm coming at them.

"Okay, killer, don't blow a gasket," Shane said. The group started moving again, weaving through the trees while the wet snow began to fall harder and faster.

The mass of black clouds was completely over the island now, and the storm was fully upon them by the time they were free of the maple trees and in the empty field between them and the village. Snow and sleet fell in such abundance that they were in nearly whiteout conditions. Shane could barely see Alina at the head of the group; she appeared as little more than a dark silhouette.

The wind howled, and it picked up through the caverns off the ocean, moaning like a great, desperate beast beneath their feet. Shane kept his eyes open for the ghost, but he saw nothing. Even if it was there, he had almost no hope of finding it. The spirit could have been pacing them the entire way.

Shane trusted Frank to keep Alina in sight and keep her safe in case anything happened. He, in turn, kept Frank in sight. If anything happened, they would serve as eyes and ears for one another to make up for the fury of the storm.

The moans grew louder. The howling of the wind was stronger than it had been any other time Shane had heard it. And as it wailed its mournful cries, he heard other sounds underneath it. A hissing at first, and then sounds like wet, guttural growls. Shane saw no shadows or movement. The men behind him were not listening and had not heard or paid attention. Frank might not have even noticed it. But it was there, hidden, and growing louder with each step. It was like the storm was stalking them. And it was hungry.

Wind gusts swirled unexpectedly, blasting from the south but then suddenly punishing them from the east for a few minutes before the southern winds returned. They were being pushed and pulled, and the cold chewed through Shane's clothing, sinking into his body as they walked.

Alina dropped back after a word from Frank, and he took point. Blaine didn't notice. The man walked with his head down to guard from the snow battering him. The girl stayed close to Shane, a scarf nearly covering her face, and followed Frank's larger footsteps in the snow.

"We went looking for you last night." The wind drowned out Shane's words almost immediately after he spoke them.

"I had to find him," she said. "I needed to see for myself."

"And?"

She looked back at him, just her eyes visible above the scarf.

"I need to leave this place." There was pleading in her words.

"That's the plan." Shane looked at Blaine to make sure the man was still ignoring them. "What happened to you? Your trail in the snow disappeared."

"What do you mean?" she asked.

"You went into the woods, and we followed. Then you vanished, no tracks anywhere. This morning, we found you in a cave with these guys after you."

Alina did not answer for a moment, and Shane thought she might not have heard or understood him over the howling wind and crunching of snow. But then, after a moment, she shook her head.

"I don't know. I found him. Jackson. And I felt so sick... I ran. I didn't know where I was, and... I don't know. The next thing I remember is waking up in that cave with a fire going."

Shane said nothing, and she returned to walking, her head down against the storm. She had either blacked out and found the cave, started a fire and gone to sleep without remembering it or someone had intervened. He needed time to puzzle that out but didn't have it.

There had to be only a short distance left before they reached the village, but the storm had stolen it from them, hiding it behind a curtain of freezing nothingness. The growls and hissing and gurgling sounds were impossible to ignore now, but it seemed as though no one else heard, or no one else understood.

In defiance of his expectations, the lights of the village were soon visible, and the ghost did not appear. Shane did not understand what game it was playing. The only thing he knew for sure was that something was being kept from him by Mallory and her people. There had to be something more, something to explain why the ghost behaved the way it did.

"That's enough," Blaine yelled as they approached the edge of the bowl, looking down over the village.

Most of the little cabins were lit with soft, yellow light coming through the windows. It was still early in the morning, but the storm made it look like evening.

Despite the raging wind, the smell of burned wood was still in the air. They were too far to the east for Shane to see the cabin, but he knew that's what he smelled. They had burned the building to the ground to murder him and Frank the night before. He thought it almost amusing that Blaine was pushing him around now as though he had some degree of control.

Shane was doing what he wanted to do. Blaine didn't know that, and he was happy to let the foolish man think he was still in control. He could go on thinking that until Shane needed him to realize something else, and then they would have words.

"Collie, head down first," Blaine said.

The unarmed man walked ahead of the others, moving past Frank and heading down the side of the shallow hill into the village itself.

"Move." Blaine forced Shane forward again and got the others to head after the man called Collie.

Shane recognized where the man in front was headed, making a beeline to Mallory's stone cabin. The barest hint of movement to the east caught Shane's eye, and he turned to look. There, only a few yards away, the ghost was crouched at the edge of the bowl. He sat like a frog, with his bony knees up, shorn of their flesh, and untouched by the snow, watching Shane with a vague curiosity.

"Frank," Shane said.

"I see him." Frank's voice was barely audible over the wind as Blaine shoved Shane from behind again, nearly knocking him down the hill.

"You can talk when someone asks you to talk," the man growled.

The snow lashed at them, whipping through the air in a fury. The wind rose, and the temperature fell. It was as though a blizzard had descended the moment they reached the border of the village.

Shane followed Alina and could no longer even see Collie in the lead. Frank was even harder to track, and the lights of the more distant cabins had faded as well.

"We gotta get inside, Blaine!" Winchester guy yelled.

"When we're done," Blaine yelled back.

"It's bad, Blaine. We—"

"When we're done!" Blaine insisted. "Keep moving."

Lights appeared ahead of them as they reached the greenhouse, the glass panels caked in snow like a giant igloo, and soon, Frank and Alina stopped moving.

Mallory appeared with maybe a half-dozen others carrying lanterns. Everyone was bundled tight against the storm, and when they shouted words, none of them made their way to Shane's ears.

Blaine pushed past Shane and Mallory caught sight of him, coming over to speak to the man. Frank and Alina were lined up next to him, and the three stood there as though being inspected by a panel while Blaine whispered in Mallory's ear.

There was some back and forth while the storm dumped snow on them with a compassionless fury, winds pelting them at blizzard strength. The village would be almost completely snowed in by the time the sun set that night.

"Alina, what have you done?" Mallory asked.

"I had to find him," she replied. "I saw what you did to him."

Mallory pulled down her scarf so that her face was visible. She frowned, accentuating the lines around her mouth and eyes, and shook her head.

"I did nothing. The island chooses and the island rewards."

"You murdered him," Alina said. "You cut the skin right off his body. Like he was an animal. A piece of meat."

"Everyone dies," Mallory said sternly. "At least here, death means something. Jackson's death made our lives better. What more could any of us hope to do in death than to improve the lives of those we leave behind?"

"You really believe that load of crap, don't you?" Shane said, drawing the woman's attention to him.

Mallory looked at him, her expression almost emotionless, but he saw the tension around her eyes and lips. She was holding back her contempt and doing a decent job of it. Even with him baiting her, she was resisting.

"You are a hollow man, aren't you, Mr. Ryan? Have you ever known a love for anything bigger than yourself? Have you ever sacrificed for the good of others instead of your enrichment? Have you ever even loved another person?"

He smiled at her and reached into his jacket. Blaine tensed, raising the rifle, and Shane chuckled as he pulled out a cigarette. Mallory scoffed openly as he struggled for a moment to light it in the wind, keeping his hands closed tightly around the end until the flame took hold, and he drew in a long, deep puff of smoke.

"You got my number, I guess," he said.

A splatter of snow hit the tip of the cigarette and snuffed it out.

"Are you done?" the woman asked.

"Looks like." Shane held up the sodden cigarette.

"Good. Blaine, kill him."

The people around Mallory tensed up. Her instructions came out of nowhere and clearly surprised the group. Even Blaine was stunned, keeping his gun steady and looking at the older woman with confusion.

"You can't!" Alina shouted, stepping forward.

Blaine reacted to her, pointing the barrel of the gun at her face and ordering her to step back.

"We have entertained this long enough," Mallory said. "These men are here to disrupt our way of life and to destroy everything we hold dear. Is that what you want?"

She was speaking to the group, turning to face the others, who were hidden behind scarves and balaclavas. Shane heard muttering, people looking at one another and speaking in hushed tones, words he could not make out.

"I have spoken to the island," Mallory said. "If these two men are allowed to leave, no one here will survive. Will you give your lives for theirs?"

"Convenient that you and the island have chats," Shane said. "Makes things easy."

Mallory turned to him again, and her expression had soured.

"Mr. Ryan… we are done talking. Blaine."

The man with the Ruger had lost some of his tough-guy bravado now that he was faced with real-life action. Nonetheless, he was emboldened with his people around him. He raised the rifle, pointing it at Shane's face. Shane looked past it at the man holding it, the barest hint of a grin curling his lips.

"You're in the big show now, huh?" Shane said.

Blaine scowled, squinting against the swirling snow. The barrel of the gun shook. Shane didn't think it was from the cold.

"Maybe we can call the cops, blame these guys for what happened to

Jackson," Blaine said.

"No!" Mallory shouted. "No one else is coming to Maple Grove. Do it!"

Winchester raised his weapon as Frank looked to take a step forward. Shane remained still. He smiled fully, and it finally set Blaine over the edge.

The barrel was point-blank between Shane's eyes when he pulled the trigger.

CHAPTER 19

DISSENTION

The gun clicked. Blaine barely had time to register surprise before Shane had pulled the barrel away and then slammed the butt into the man's face. It crushed the bridge of Blaine's nose, breaking it, and knocking the man unconscious. He fell to the ground in a heap, bleeding into the snow while the others screamed in panic, several running now that they saw Shane was armed.

Mallory stood her ground, her face a cold fury with only a hint of confusion. Shane held the gun up while Winchester shakily turned on Shane, far too panicked to pull the trigger.

"Ruger's a one-shot rifle. Oughta tell your boy to reload if he plans any public executions," Shane said, tossing the gun into a pile of snow.

"Mallory, you can't do this!" One of her people shouted to be heard over the moaning wind.

Winchester looked ready to cut and run until Frank distracted him. He brought his rifle to bear, and Shane snatched the barrel from him as well, letting him go without the blow to the face but disarming him and unloading the weapon before tossing it into the snow.

More of the villagers argued as others ventured from their homes and into the snow to see what was happening. Mallory's eyes focused on Shane, as cold as the snow that blew around them.

"You will never get off this island," she told him. "I will not let you destroy this place."

Even as she spoke, Shane's attention was drawn away. He had no doubt she would bluster at him, rage in her way, and she would believe herself right. But something else was happening.

A shadow moved in the snow past the nearest cabins, skulking about in the gray where it could barely be seen. Too thin to be one of the villagers, and not burdened by clothing. The ghost had crept closer and was circling like a wolf after weakened prey. It looked like the spirit was biding its time, maybe looking for the right opportunity to strike. But at what target?

"I found Jackson in the woods," Alina said suddenly, loudly, to draw everyone's attention. "He didn't leave. He never went home. Someone dumped him out there and butchered him. His body was cut apart like he wasn't even a person."

"Alina!" Mallory snapped.

The younger woman glared at her and shook her head.

"Mallory is a liar, and she is a killer! Jackson was good. He was a good person, and he didn't deserve that."

The chatter among the villagers was a drone that joined the moaning wind. They were not all on Mallory's side as Frank had thought. They had been told that Jackson left the island, or a wholesome tale of going back to nature, or whatever Mallory fed them to keep them content and in the dark.

"You are a foolish girl, and you have no idea what you're talking about," Mallory said.

"This is over," Shane interrupted her. "Whatever deal you made with the ghost, your island spirit, it's over."

Mallory backed up as some of her followers helped Blaine to his feet. The bottom half of the man's face was awash in blood. His nose was crooked, and bruises were already forming around his eyes. They'd be black by the next day.

The ranks of Maple Grove were being divided. Mallory had those still loyal to her, the ones who probably knew all along what had happened to Jackson. The rest were now unsure, scared of the sudden turn to violence and revelations from Alina. They left in groups, abandoning the greenhouse and their leader to whatever she had planned. They might not have been on board with her, but they were not willing to stand against her.

Shane did not want the villagers around and was glad to see them leave. Better they hide in their homes than take a stand one way or the other. They would get themselves killed if they weren't careful.

The ghost had vanished again, hidden behind the cabins and in the storm.

Blaine shook off the help of the people who got him to his feet, wiping his bloody nose on the back of his sleeve and scowling at Shane.

Frank took a step forward then, putting himself between Shane and Blaine. Shane wasn't sure why at first, but then he saw that Blaine's hand had slipped into his belt. He pulled out a knife, the kind that was used for carving wood or some small task, but still sharp enough to do damage.

"Blaine, there's no reason to do something you might regret," Frank said.

Blaine didn't respond. Instead, he came at Frank, blade extended. Frank sidestepped the attack easily enough. Blaine was clumsy, and his weapon was not meant for fighting. As soon as Frank was out of the way, Shane grabbed Blaine by the wrist and twisted his arm behind him, squeezing and pushing down at the same time.

The other man struggled but only briefly. Shane's grip was strong, and once he put pressure on Blaine's twisted arm, the other man relaxed his grip immediately and dropped the knife. It fell into the fresh snow, and Shane, behind him now, released him with a kick in the back that knocked him face-first to the ground.

Blaine struggled to his feet, his anger far outweighing any common sense, ready for a third try, when someone screamed. Others followed, and panic broke out as even Mallory's loyalists fled.

The ghost had crept from the shadows between cabins, and everyone could see him now. Blood flowed from the numerous wounds and scraps of flesh that clung to his body, leaving a crimson trail through the snow wherever he went. Even Mallory seemed stunned by his presence, and Blaine all but forgot about Shane as he stumbled backward, gibbering incoherently as he looked at the spirit with dread.

"Everybody, go back to your homes, quickly!" Frank raised his hands to get people's attention though the terrified screams were still much louder.

Shane took Blaine by the collar and looked the man square in the eyes.

"If you want to live, you need to get everyone out of here," he said.

He pushed him back, not waiting to see if the man would comply, and turned on the ghost that stalked toward the loosely assembled group of people. Frank had already sent Alina on her way and was getting some of the less-rational others to do as he said. Only Mallory stood her ground, silent and unafraid, as Shane approached the spirit.

"One more time?" Shane asked.

The ghost had nothing to say, but it obliged him. The two met in the center of the snow-filled road, the ghost using the advantage of not being encumbered by the snow to slip low and pull Shane's leg out from under him.

Shane landed softly, the snow being good for something, but cursed as the ghost was on him almost immediately. The spirit did not have to worry about the cold or the weather; he passed through the freezing air as if it weren't there, giving him an advantage of speed and agility.

They rolled together, and Shane tossed his gloves aside. He needed his hands to grip and attack the ghost, but the cold would wear him down fast. He needed to be faster.

Their previous encounter had not lasted long. Shane had learned a bit of the spirit's fighting style, but not enough to put up a solid defense or a counter-offensive. He fared better this time than he had in the woods. He was ready for the slick and quick attacks the ghost employed, and the sneaky way he bent and moved due to the condition of his body.

When the ghost slipped behind him, Shane's elbow caught him in the jaw, cracking a tooth loose and causing the ghost to stumble back. He shook his head like a boxer clearing the haze and came at Shane again. No sound, and barely a delay. The ghost was nothing if not determined and efficient.

Mallory watched with growing frustration. Shane suspected she expected the ghost to kill him quickly, make short work of him, and put an end to what she considered to be her problem. She had not expected Shane to fight back.

The street has been emptied of nearly everyone. Only Frank and Mallory remained watching Shane fight. Even Blaine had taken the warning to heart and cleared out, taking whatever stragglers were there with him.

Frank stood near Mallory, watching her and Shane as the fight progressed. Shane focused on the ghost but stayed aware of Mallory's location as much as he could be. He wouldn't put it past her to find the Winchester and take Shane out.

The blizzard became more furious, the snowfall not just pounding down from above but from the south, the east, and even the north.

The wind was fierce and biting. Shane felt a sting in his knuckles and flexed his fingers whenever he pulled away from the spirit before sparring with him again, capturing attacks as best he could and getting some advantage. The worse the snow got, the less likely it seemed that Shane would get the upper hand.

The ghost had steadily backed away, leading Shane toward a road between cabins. He had thought perhaps at first that he was just losing ground, but now Shane was certain the ghost was doing it intentionally. He baited him, squared off with him, and then when he had a chance to press the offensive, he stepped back and let Shane take him, moving them farther and farther from the greenhouse and Mallory.

Shane was careful in his pacing. If the ghost was luring him into a trap, he wasn't going to go so easily. He backed off, took hold of the ghost, and threw him back the way they had come. For the first time, his attack elicited a sound from the spirit. A growl, nothing more, but it sounded frustrated.

"Getting tired?" Shane asked.

The ghost offered no response, but a noise behind him drew his attention. He moved with the ghost until he saw Blaine reappear from the cabin next to Mallory's with Winchester and two more men. They were all armed with rifles, and Blaine had a new look of resolve.

He was ready to kill now.

CHAPTER 20
BEYOND THE STORM

"Shane," Frank shouted in warning.

Shane nodded as Frank crossed the clearing away from Blaine and the other men. He ducked behind Shane and the ghost, crossing the small intersection in which they'd all found themselves.

"This way, quickly." Alina appeared at a second street on Shane's left. She was covered by the houses, out of sight of Mallory and the men, but visible to Shane and Frank.

The ghost pushed off Shane and backed up, then backed away again, sidestepping Frank and fading into the snow between two cabins. Someone fired a shot from next to Mallory's house, and Shane ducked while Frank ran past him. The bullet ricocheted off a stone hut, and Shane heard it whiz by his head. Still bad shots, but closer than the last time. It was time to go.

Shane and Frank fled into the alley, joining Alina and leaving the others while the ghost remained hidden somewhere in the falling snow and shadow. The men were reluctant to cross over to the street, fearful that the spirit was waiting for them.

"You see where he went?" Shane asked.

"Gone," Frank said. "No idea."

Alina was already running, not interested in the conversation, and Shane didn't blame her. He followed close behind with Frank at his side, ducking past cabins, to the bright green door of her place.

"We can't hide in here," Shane said to her as she opened her door to lead them in. "This is the first place they'll look."

"I know." She closed the door behind them.

The inside of her cabin was warm and full of blown-glass ornaments and decorations that she must have made. They reflected the light from her fire a thousand times over and made the space glitter.

"I've got blankets and matches and things you can take. You have to get out of here," she said.

She was half-frantic, grabbing things from a small closet and pushing them into a backpack. Shane wanted to tell her not to worry about it, but with the blizzard outside, they would need more than just their coats.

The sugar shack would be the first place anyone looked for them. Aside from that, Shane hadn't seen another building on the island. That meant they would have to fend for themselves against the elements. And against the ghost.

Shane and Frank helped her pack up. There wasn't much, just a couple of sturdy blankets, some food and water, a small hatchet, and waterproof matches. They moved quickly because Blaine and the others would not be far behind. Fear of the ghost would be the only thing holding them at bay, and when they realized it was gone, they would pursue the duo.

"You should come with us," Frank said.

Alina shook her head.

"They won't hurt me. Mallory's angry, but she won't do anything. And I need to convince the others to get out of here. She betrayed our trust. Jackson is dead because of her."

She paused then, turning away from Shane long enough to take a deep breath and steady herself.

"There's a door out the back. Head straight, and you'll make it up to the northern edge of the island. If you follow the rocks, you can get back around to the sugar shack or the cave if you can make it."

"Thank you, Alina." Frank took her hand before heading to the back door. "Please stay safe."

"I will," she said.

Shane shouldered the pack and pulled a stocking cap over his head, putting his gloves back on before he opened the door. The blizzard was in full force, and swirling white had replaced the landscape.

There was no sign of Blaine or the other armed men behind Alina's cabin. Not that Shane would have seen them if they were more than ten feet away. The upside to that was Shane and Frank were just as invisible to their hunters. Even tracking them through the snow would be impossible in a matter of minutes.

Frank took the lead, cutting a path from Alina's door to the edge of the village. The bowl that surrounded them was much shallower on this end of the town. They climbed what was barely a small hill until they were in what looked like an endless, white field. Shane knew they were near the island's edge, and if they continued straight for much longer, they would reach the southern coastline. There was nothing there for them, no place to shelter or keep safe from their pursuers.

The spectral howling of the wind was worse than it had been only moments earlier. Through his feet, Shane felt the rock of the island vibrating with the mournful hum and groans. He was still not sure if it was a natural phenomenon or something the ghost was causing.

Shane was having trouble wrapping his head around the ghost's motivations. The ghost had to have saved Alina from dying in the woods, and he also could have easily continued the fight with Shane in town, but he backed off when the gunman approached. In Shane's mind, it seemed like he allowed Shane and Frank to escape. But it didn't make sense.

Even though Shane wore gloves and a hat, the storm battered Shane as he signaled to Frank, and they circled the village to the east. The whiteout conditions provided them ample cover, and he doubted Blaine or the others would have the skill or desire to track them. If they had started again, they likely would have just looked through the cabins and then given up.

Despite her belief that she would be fine, Shane worried about Alina.

Mallory had proven more willing to kill than any of them suspected. If Alina had come with them, though, she would have been at just as much risk. Shane could protect her from people, but she didn't have the skill to be out in harsh weather and fighting for her life. He had to take her at her word that she'd be safer in town.

"We can't survive in this." Frank drew close to Shane to talk, his voice nearly drowned out by the wind through the subterranean passages.

Shane nodded. Frank was right. No matter where they ventured, they would die in that storm. Without shelter, if it didn't let up, they had no hope. The temperature had dropped considerably. The cold stung Shane's exposed flesh and found ways to creep through the seams of his clothes.

Instead of answering, Shane pointed to the village, where dim flashes of light appeared irregularly. They were moving, fading into the storm, and then appearing again elsewhere, moments later. Flashlights. A search party looking for something. Blaine and his men.

It was as Shane expected. The men were searching the village. They were probably heading from cabin to cabin and would search everyone. No doubt they had started with Alina and were frustrated when they found nothing there.

The two of them crouched together, close to the southeastern edge of the bowl where it started to rise higher above the rooftops of the cabins. There was minimal cover there thanks to a handful of shrubs, but the visibility meant no one would see them unless they were almost standing.

The darting lights were the only indication that there was anything in the village besides shadows and tricks of the eye caused by the movement of the barrage of snow. They watched the lights progress, mapping the invisible village along the unpaved roads.

"You want to get back into town and hide out after the search ends?" Frank asked.

"Think it's our best bet," Shane said.

"Not necessarily," Frank said. "What about the boats?"

Shane glanced at the other man and then returned his eyes to the village and the irregular flashing lights.

"You think we can get one out of here?"

"Maybe," Frank said. "We can certainly alert the authorities to this place, or at least contact Mo and make up a solid plan to get out of here. I can tell Jackson's father what happened. And we can get out of the storm and stay warm for a night without risking capture."

"We can't leave," Shane said.

"Shane."

Frank went silent until Shane looked him in the eye.

"Jackson's dead. We almost got burned alive. I'm not asking you to walk away from this fight, but we cannot police this whole island. This is not what either of us do. These people are killers. Even if the ghost is involved, we can make a move on that when the time is right. But we can't let Mallory and her loyalists terrorize a village of innocent people."

Shane said nothing for a moment, considering his friend's words. He nodded as he watched the obscured flashes of light moving about below them. Frank was right, of course. It wasn't his job to catch killers this way. If they could find a place to hole up for the night and wait out the blizzard, he knew they could get the upper hand. They could take out Mallory, Blaine, and anyone else on the island who worked with the ghost. But Frank was right.

It was too much to overthrow a village of people. They had come to learn whether a young man was alive or dead, and they had their answer. Sticking around could get people like Alina or Clint hurt.

Shane hated turning his back on a fight, but he couldn't look at it that way. He wasn't giving up. The real fight was with the ghost; the rest could be someone else's fight. The police, if Frank wanted to get them involved. Frank had been called in officially to investigate; he could handle those explanations. Shane would step back and let that happen, and then later, when the coast was clear, nothing would be between him and the ghost.

"Okay," Shane said. "No one will expect us to leave in this storm, anyway."

The blizzard would make a good cover for a getaway. On the other hand, leaving in the storm was a bad idea for all the obvious reasons. Neither he nor Frank had been a sailor, but Shane could hold his own on a boat. He hoped Frank had some sea legs if he planned to leave under such conditions.

Shane stood, and he and Frank walked around the outside of the village until they were far enough away to hook to the west and head toward the docks. There was no trail to follow, and he was guessing distance and direction based on the map he had created in his mind. They would likely need to search along the western edge of the island for the path to the ocean.

Shane and Frank didn't speak. They marched, heads down, into the wind. The distance seemed longer than it should have, but their path was off the mark due to the weather, adding yards to the journey that passed at a snail's pace in shin-deep snow.

The gray horizon became clear in time, and the stony wall that led to the western shore and docks. They were farther south than they intended and followed the wall north, looking for the narrow trail they had ascended on the first day.

They heard the waves crashing on the rocks, and soon enough, Shane had a view, however fleeting, of what looked like the docks. He held out a hand to stop Frank before they got too close. Ahead of them, at the top of the trail, two men from the village stood holding rifles, bundled up against the cold.

"We've got a problem," Shane whispered.

CHAPTER 21
THE HEART OF ICE

There was no way to tell who the two men guarding the trail down to the docks were. Shane didn't think they were Blaine's men, though. There was no way they could have gotten there in time, and from the look of them, they had been stationed in the blizzard for a while.

"I didn't think there would be guards," Frank whispered.

They were crouched behind a patch of shrubs no more than ten yards from the guards, but the snow obscured them.

"Maybe they'll freeze to death, and we can use their corpses like toboggans," Shane suggested.

Frank frowned at him, and Shane shrugged.

"Just an idea."

"I don't want to wait that long. We could just disarm them. Doubt either is expecting a fight."

Shane nodded. They had been watching the men, one of whom sat on a tree stump, the other on a rock. He wondered how Mallory had convinced them to stay out in such a storm or how long they were expected to endure it. Her people had faith if nothing else.

"Didn't think you'd be up for fighting," Shane said. "Peaceful resolutions and all that."

"Again, they did try to burn us alive," Frank said. "And I think it'd be a greater mercy to take them out and send them running home now so they can get some of that awful tea and warm up."

"Mercy beating," Shane said. "I can get behind that."

Frank shifted position in the snow, putting out a hand to steady himself, ready to start into as much of a run as could be achieved in the snow.

"I go right, you go left," he said.

"Call it," Shane agreed.

"Go."

They got up from behind the snow-laden scrub, rushing toward the guards like monsters born from the storm. Shane made a beeline for the man sitting on the tree stump, intending to tackle the man into the snow and relieve him of his weapon.

"They're here!" Frank's target yelled.

Instead of preparing for the fight, the man lifted his arm, and a blast of bright red shot up into the sky. He'd fired an emergency flare.

Blinding red filled the air. The blowing snow looked like a swirling storm of blood clots as the flare ascended below the low clouds and scorched the sky.

Frank tackled him with a sturdy shoulder to the gut, and Shane was on his man before he even realized what his partner was doing. Somewhere beneath a scarf and a balaclava, the man groaned in pain as Shane landed on top of him.

The rifle was tossed to one side, and Shane pressed his forearm across his throat.

"Please don't kill me," the man begged, muffled and pathetic. Shane grunted, his enthusiasm for a fight waning in the face of a man who had already given up.

Next to him, Frank wrestled with his target in the snow. They rolled over, and Frank landed a series of kidney punches that had their thunder stolen by layers of padded winter coat.

"That flare meant to bring backup?" Shane asked.

"Yes! Mallory made us wait here for you. We just had to call for help. My gun's not even loaded!"

Shane sighed, holding the man down and waiting for Frank to subdue the other man.

"You alright over there?" he asked.

Frank had rolled the man face-down in the snow and was kneeling on the small of his back. His breath rolled out in great, steaming clouds that were whipped away swiftly by the blowing snow.

"Doing fine, thanks."

He looked back the way they had come. There was nothing there, nothing to see more than a few yards off. The flare had been bright. It could have been seen from the village through the storm.

If Blaine and the others were coming, the time they had to descend the hill and steal a boat was limited. Too limited. In that weather, without even knowing if they could get a boat started, it was a fool's plan. They'd be trapping themselves in a corner.

"We have to get into the forest," Shane said.

It was the only place where they could lose their pursuers and maybe find a spot to rest and consider their next option. Mallory and the others would know they were making a play for the boats. They might bulk up security, but Shane didn't have a lot of faith that they could hold out for long if the storm didn't subside. That could be their option. Just being able to wait it out better than the locals.

"You should go back to the village before you freeze to death. It's not worth it." Shane got up off the man he had tackled.

He picked up the rifle with him and hurled it off the edge of the cliff, looking down to the side after it. The snow had swallowed everything. The path was lost; he couldn't even see the docks from where he stood to know the condition of the boats or how easy it would be to commandeer one.

Frank was on his feet as well, and they left the villagers behind in the snow and headed toward the maple forest.

"We're going to find you!" the man Frank had subdued yelled after them.

He quickly descended into an argument with the other man over why he hadn't done enough to fight back, but their words were swallowed by the wind. Frank and Shane were gone from sight just as quickly.

Shane had little faith in the man's threat. But that didn't mean Shane and Frank were safe. The cold was brutal, the temperature continued to drop, and he already felt it penetrating through the layers he wore. They needed to find a cave, or at least a ravine or some other sheltered area to hunker down and wait out the storm.

Mallory was willing to put guards at risk to protect the places they knew Shane and Frank would go to. That was fine. It had been easy enough to take out those two men; they could take out anyone else who was set against them as well. No one on the island seemed like a good shot, and very few seemed to even have the will to follow through. Mallory would not get what she wanted.

Frank took the lead through the trees, setting a good pace despite the poor conditions. He cut east quickly, and they investigated any depressions or slightly protected areas they found along the route. Nothing offered the kind of cover they needed. Nothing stood up to the blizzard, which seemed to come from all directions at once.

There was an option to make a shelter, to build something out of snow, but Shane didn't want to risk the time it would take. Instead, they continued toward where they had found Alina and the others earlier in the day. The cave she had been in offered good coverage, and if anyone came to find them, they would have to walk down the narrow path one at a time. It gave Shane and Frank the best option for defense and protection from the elements.

The shelter of the cave would give them the chance to start a fire that wouldn't be seen readily by others as well. Even with the blankets and other gear Alina had given them, they needed fire to survive if they were going to stay outside for another day, or however long it took for them to get to the boats.

The howls of the wind through the caverns below the ground seemed louder in the forest. They were halfway across the island when their progress slowed considerably. The drifts between the trees had built up, rising like frozen waves caused by the tree trunks splitting the snow and forcing it to pile up unevenly.

Frank walked with his head down, trudging toward their unseen goal. Shane kept his eyes open for the ghost. The wet snow, propelled by gale-force winds, splattered him in the face every time he looked around. Even with a hand raised to shield himself, it was hard to look up for any length of time. Not that it mattered. The ghost could have been two feet away, and he never would have seen it.

They were on the dead man's turf, and the ghost had all the advantages. The weather would not slow him, the snow would not blind him, and nothing was stopping him from attacking whenever he wanted.

The wind changed direction again. It had blasted them from the east and then, with a quick twist, it suddenly battered them from the north. The freezing wind became even colder, and the men changed in the direction they held their heads, adjusting to keep their faces clear.

In the fraction of a moment it took Shane to twist his neck and look to one side, Frank was gone.

He stopped and scanned the forest in front of him.

"Frank?" The storm ripped the words from his mouth and smothered them. "Frank!"

He rushed forward, looking around the tree that Frank had been next to seconds earlier. The man was not there. Shane turned in a circle, walking around the largest snowbanks on either side of him. There was nothing.

"Frank!"

A guttural cry reached Shane's ears. He turned and saw Frank several yards away, barely visible, being dragged through the snow to the north.

Shane ran, the snow and wind battering him in the face. The ground was uneven; frozen mud in some parts and piled high with snow in others. He saw Frank crest one of the snowbanks, and the ghost, crouched low, dragging him by the ankle.

The ghost moved quickly, pulling Frank as if he weighed nothing. Frank struggled to right himself, to get the opportunity to even reach his ankle to strike the spirit with one of his iron rings, but it was impossible. With the speed of the ghost and the unevenness of the ground, it was all Frank could do to lift his head or grab at a branch to steady himself.

Unhindered by the weather though the ghost might have been, it was limited in how quickly and easily it could move now that it was anchored to Frank. That gave Shane the advantage. He ran without caution, taking more risks than he normally would over such uneven ground, nearly tripping and righting himself several times until he caught up.

Shane grabbed Frank by the wrist, digging in the heels of his boots and forcing the ghost to lurch to a stop. The ghost looked back at Shane and chattered his teeth. With an almost absentminded movement, the spirit jerked Frank to one side, rolling him down a slight embankment into a large drift of snow on their right.

With Frank out of the way, the ghost clacked his teeth together slowly and loudly, almost shaking his head for a moment like he was disappointed. Shane no longer cared what the ghost was up to or why it did the things that it did. He pulled off his gloves, flexed his fingers in the cold air, and ran at him.

CHAPTER 22

THE EATEN

The ghost met Shane without hesitation. His bony arms felt like they were made of fat-smeared metal, and though they didn't absorb the cold of the surrounding air, the ghost was frozen enough that it felt like Shane was grappling with icicles.

Aside from random teeth chatters, the spirit refused to make any noise or communicate. He still fought defensively. There were moments when the ghost could have advanced, capitalized, or followed through better, but he did not. Something about it enraged Shane even further and made him fight harder, attempting to break one of the fleshless arms more than once but falling short each time.

Whenever Shane got a grip on something—a humerus, a femur, anything that had been shaved down to the bone—the ghost wriggled free almost instantly. His body was slick and slippery in the cold, and it was nearly impossible to capture him in a submission hold or something powerful enough to cripple him.

Shane switched tactics, realizing he would not gain the upper hand by grabbing the ghost to destroy like he might under other circumstances. Instead, he threw punches.

Fists collided with the ghost's exposed jaw. When Shane got the chance, he went in with an elbow or a knee. He didn't try any follow-through; no grappling or holding the ghost firmly. The ghost was ready for those maneuvers and countered them too easily. Instead, Shane parried and struck again, aiming for somewhere else to throw the ghost off-track.

The ghost shook off most of the blows. The sludgy layer that covered every exposed surface caused even Shane's hardest punches to glance off. Very few seemed direct or damaging, and even then, they would have only bruised a living man and did little permanent damage to the spirit.

It did not take long for the ghost to adjust his fighting style to Shane's new strategy. When Shane threw a punch, the ghost dropped back through a snowbank or a log, places Shane couldn't follow without crossing over or through a roadblock, costing him reach that took power out of his blows.

The snow and wind swirled around them, and Shane felt his body temperature rise. He needed to remain calm and conserve his energy. He had to be smart and strategic, but the ghost was not doing what Shane needed him to do.

Instead of advancing, Shane backed off. The ghost watched him, chattered his teeth, and then advanced slowly. Now, Shane was on the defensive. It was purely to see how the ghost would react, to see what the spirit would do if Shane refused to bring the fight to him.

He backed away, coming close to a ridge in the forest that led down a steep shrub-and-root-covered hill that had been mostly shielded from the snow at the top by overhanging trees. Farther down, where the ground evened out, it looked like a blank canvas.

The defensive tactic was less effective than Shane had hoped. The weather and the landscape prevented him from backing up as much or as quickly as he wanted. The ridge bound him in on one side, and the snow slowed him all around. He couldn't easily spar with the ghost, dance around him, and keep him on his toes.

He had given Frank enough time to climb out of the ravine where he had been dropped and recover from the attack he had endured. Several yards separated the two men, and Shane was debating the best way to approach the ghost when he heard a noise in the distance.

It was nothing he could make out clearly, and it was mostly drowned out by the howling of the wind, but it was a distinctly human voice.

Someone was out there yelling. The people from the village had seen the flare and responded.

There was no way to know how many men Mallory had sent. Shane doubted she could have gotten more than ten people to head out. Most did not seem to want to embrace her methods, but enough of them did.

The ghost capitalized on the distraction, coming at Shane through the snowdrifts, grasping him by the front of the coat, and lifting him off the ground.

Frank was running toward him, silent to not alert the villagers, but he was too late. The ghost hurled Shane from the ridge, tossing him into the air like a rag doll and past the trees to the steep slope.

Shane hit hard, crashing into skeletal shrubs and gnarled roots on the hillside before rolling end over end. He couldn't slow himself; the momentum and steep angle prevented him from gaining his footing or orientation.

Frozen jags of stone and branches tore at Shane's clothing, some of them digging into his neck, his face, and the backs of his legs as he tumbled down the ridge into the snow-filled clearing below. When he finally stopped, he was buried a foot below the snow with only a hole in the shape of his body above him showing the swirling, gray sky.

The numbing cold prevented him from feeling the sharpness of the pain right away. He felt spots of blood freezing along his legs and face. Nothing was too serious; he hadn't broken or permanently damaged anything, but he was badly bruised, and his clothing was torn. Numerous scrapes stung in the subzero temperatures and biting wind as he clawed his way out of the deep drift into which he'd been thrown.

Frank waved at him from above, keeping silent as he indicated his intention to climb down. The ghost was gone, and Shane made a signal inquiring. Frank shook his head. The ghost had squandered another opportunity for a kill.

Shane waved Frank off and pointed east, his intention to meet the other man farther down rather than have Frank waste time climbing down. They needed to get away from the villagers, and time was precious.

Frank nodded and disappeared above the ridge. Shane climbed out of the snow to the hill's base, where he got better footing and shook himself off. The pack Alina gave him was not far away, snagged on a root, and he grabbed it again.

The plan was to forge ahead, reach the place where the hills evened out, and rejoin Frank. They would have to be close to the eastern cliffs, and getting to the caves would only be a matter of following the wall.

Shouting voices came to Shane over the ridgeline, and he stopped and pulled back, bringing his body tight against the base of the hill where it would be harder to see him from the top. He heard them as they approached, someone shouting about tracks. They must have seen where Frank was dragged or where Shane had squared off with the ghost. The snow inside the forest covered things up slower, so they were vulnerable to being tracked.

When the voices lowered, Shane heard nothing. Sometimes a hint of something, a single word, or the muffled sound of voices came down to him, but nothing useful. It did not sound like they had found Frank, nor had they seen him where he waited.

"We'll find you," a voice shouted into the storm.

Shane recognized Blaine's voice, more smug than the last time they'd talked. There was cruelness to Blaine that belied his presence in a syrup-producing hippie commune on the sea. He didn't cling to the idea of peace and love nearly as well as everyone else. Even Mallory held up the idea that she was working for the greater good. Blaine was just a small man, a bully who had found an outlet for his anger.

Shane was content to wait Blaine and the others out, but by the time they started moving, it was clear they were heading east. They were following the path Frank had likely left when he headed in that direction. Shane could not risk following from below the ridge and being seen or running into them once he reached the eastern wall.

Frank no doubt would have taken cover or changed direction to evade them. He would improvise as much as Shane would, and there was no way to know where he had gone. They would have to meet up later when it was safe.

He gave the villagers several minutes to put some distance between themselves and his hiding place and then doubled back, heading west and looking for a safe place to climb up again.

The hill evened out, and the ridge smoothed over until it was just a slight incline. Near the end where the forest came together again, he found an upturned tree that looked as though it had fallen decades ago. The underside of it had created a hollow like a cavern of wood and root, and inside, several skulls had been placed.

The blowing snow reached the hollow but just barely. The skulls were mostly uncovered, some of them staked out on a short length of wood and others piled haphazardly. There were dozens. No other bones, just the skulls.

One of the skulls had a gold tooth, and many others were missing a significant number of teeth. It didn't look like they had fallen out after death. The jaws looked like they had grown for some time without the teeth as though the people they belonged to had endured a history of poor dental health. They were old. Well more than one hundred years. And several had clear signs of bite marks. The jawbone of the skull with the golden tooth had a deep imprint on it. Someone had clamped down hard on the bone once upon a time.

Shane crouched in front of the skulls and looked around. How long had the ghost been on the island? How long had he fed on people, if not literally, then in his mind? And who had killed him in the first place?

The mystery of the spirit was getting to him, presenting Shane with new questions but no answers. If this thing had cannibalized people on the island for more than a century, why was it playing so coy with Shane now?

It should have been well into its routine.

He knew ghosts were creatures of habit. They were forced to be, for the most part. They had a limited range and options. Whether haunting a house or an island, ghosts only did certain things, and they did them repetitively. If this ghost had a long history of killing and eating people, what was it playing at now?

He left the pile of skulls behind and circled the hollow, up the hill, and back toward where he had been thrown down. The blizzard continued to rage and visibility was low. Still, Shane knew he could sneak up on Blaine and the others without them seeing him.

And he needed to find Frank.

CHAPTER 23
THE RING

Frank nodded, understanding Shane's signal, and headed east along the ridgeline. The hill Shane had been thrown down was too steep, it looked like a landslide might have occurred long ago and pulled down part of the forest. Wherever the land leveled out was lost to the storm ahead of him. It could have been twenty yards or one hundred, but at some point, there had to be a place where their paths would meet up.

The ghost had vanished again. Frank was ready with his hands exposed, iron rings already numbing his fingers in the biting cold, but he was gone. Frank had expected him to follow Shane over the ledge or to come back for Frank now that he was alone, but he seemed to have abandoned them.

Frank had made barely any progress through the trees when a shout rang out behind him. Frank crouched behind one of the maples, watching through the flurries as a lantern light fought against the swirling storm.

He stayed out of sight, waiting to see who was coming and where they were headed. There were multiple men, shouting at one another to be heard over the storm. The signal flare had been seen in the village, and they were in pursuit.

Someone yelled something about tracks, and Frank saw the dim lantern light move. Others followed it, three that he noticed. One of the voices was Blaine's.

Frank stayed low, using trees and snow drift as cover. He knew the men could not see him in the storm and he began to flank them, keeping them in sight as best he could. He could do little about leaving tracks in the snow, but the blowing wind would take care of them soon enough. If they stumbled upon any, he wanted to make sure they led away from Shane.

Even though his friend had indicated that he was okay, Frank doubted that Shane took the fall without injury. He wasn't one to complain about a broken bone or bleeding wounds; he would just consider those an inconvenience. The medic in Frank knew better, though. Shane needed time to recover, and if Frank couldn't give him that, he would at least do his best to ensure that Shane didn't need to run for his life.

Frank continued to circle wide of the men from the village, leaving the clear enough trail through the snow and heading west once he got behind them. He watched the progress of their lanterns and listened to their shouts about tracks and signs of a fight. They had stumbled on the place where Shane had fought the ghost.

Hidden behind a tree, Frank waited until he heard more shouting. They had found his trail and were abandoning the ridge, no longer looking for Shane but following him.

Frank put his gloves back on and stayed crouched on the western side of a pair of trees growing close together. Although the storm swirled inside the forest, the western side was getting the least amount of it. Trees leaning in that direction were often covered by small snowbanks on their eastern or northern sides, with exposed soil and leaves on the west. Frank kept his feet planted there and used the trees to support himself, moving from one to the next, and stepping in the dirt rather than in the snow.

His path was haphazard and nonsensical, following only which trees he could reach from the tree before, but his trail had stopped several yards earlier. With the still-blowing snow, it would be nearly impossible for Blaine and the others to pick it up again. Even then, they would need a tracker with some amount of skill to find the barely noticeable signs Frank left behind.

He worked quickly, ensuring that there was enough space between where his trail ended and where he was, so that none of the men could see him even if they caught up. He used the storm as cover and then abandoned his obfuscation to continue westward.

Frank knew he would have to go east again at some point. He would meet up with Shane where they had agreed, but he didn't want to lead the others in that direction if he didn't have to. He had time to circle wide; he was well-insulated against the cold and could last a while longer.

The light from the lanterns and the other men's voices faded quickly, and Frank was alone once again. He kept his eyes and his ears open, looking and listening for anything out of the ordinary.

Frank knew the ghost could take advantage of the landscape much better than he could. When he had attacked him earlier, dragging him away by the ankle, Frank had not even seen the ghost.

Frank racked his brain for the reason the ghost had not killed him or Shane when he had the upper hand. Not just in the forest, but in the village. He had tried to speak with him, but he had shown no interest in communication. That left him baffled. Mallory had obviously found a way to communicate. They had struck some kind of deal, but none of it made sense to him.

The performative act of cannibalism was something unique. He had never heard of another ghost doing that. The spirit looked to have suffered a similar fate, so Frank saw the link, but that seemed to imply a lack of rationality. Any ghost that would behave like that was usually not keen on making deals.

While Frank weaved through the trees, the storm's fury lessened, and he found himself in a small clearing. The snowfall was light, just barely covering the circle of stones that had been arranged in the center of the small space. He had come back to the clearing lined with gravestones.

It was hard to judge direction in the blizzard, even to guess where he was, relative to things like the coast or the village, but Frank knew he was in the wrong place. The ring of stones should have been farther east. It should have been close to the ravine where he'd found Jackson's body, but Frank was positive he was nowhere near that. Nevertheless, the ring was there.

Frank waited at the edge of the ring, standing next to a tree as though he might blend in with it. He scanned the clearing and the circle of trees around it. No ghost watched him, and nothing crept about in the shadows or the swirling snow.

Carefully, Frank stepped out into the clearing. He moved as though he thought he might be spraying a trap at any moment, but nothing happened, and after several steps, he was committed to the action and emboldened to go forward with more purpose.

The stones were covered with only a light coating of snow. He brushed off the first and looked down at it, seeing the cross etched into the rock. To the side, almost where the rock curved down to the ground, was another mark. Three simple vertical slashes. They were hastily made, with the sharp edge of another stone or maybe a knife.

The next rock had the same cross and then, again, close to the curve of the rock and piled under snow and leaves was the second mark. A vertical scrape and then one that split into a V. The Roman numeral four.

Frank went around the circle, clearing them all. The numbers one through seven were scraped into the rocks, usually right at the edge where the rock curved down as though someone wrote it there as a reminder and not a true marker for others to take notice of.

Frank knew they were grave markers. Seven bodies were buried in a circle in the middle of the forest, who knew how long ago. He wondered if the ghost was one of them or the one who had killed them. If the ghost had been the killer, who buried them? And how long ago? The stones looked like they had been there for quite a long time.

"Please, if you're there, just tell me what you want."

He spoke to no one. There was no way to know if the ghost was around, but it was worth the effort. So far, in Frank's experience with the ghost, the situation had always been a frantic one with other people. He had not had a chance to communicate on his own or to learn anything about the ghost and what he wanted.

Every time Frank went to work, it was a risk. There was no way to know how a ghost would react until it reacted. He and Shane approached their jobs differently, but the danger was often the same. Shane was just more well-equipped to handle the problem if it turned out that a fight was the only solution.

Frank was always afraid, fear twisting in his guts each time he dealt with the unknown. He didn't let it slow him down, but he didn't ignore it. He had to compartmentalize that fear every time, acknowledging it and then setting it aside to worry about later. It was the only way he could get through any job.

Sometimes, it was unnecessary. Sometimes, the spirit was just lonely, confused, or lost. Those were the jobs that kept him going, where he felt like his gift made a difference and that he was helping people, not just the living but those who had passed on.

Maple Grove was another matter. He had hoped that he could help his friend, that he could find Jackson, and send him home to his father. When that failed, he hoped he could at least communicate with the spirit and find out the reason the young man had died, so he could offer his father some solace or understanding. But Frank had none of that. The island gave him nothing.

"I just want to understand," Frank said. "I want to help."

The only answer he received was from the wind. That strange howling that came from underground, whaling through cracks in unseen caverns, making the island sound like it was suffering.

Frustrated, Frank stood, leaving the ring of gravestones behind. He looked around the clearing, deciding to move northwest. He started his circle there, heading up and around and then finally back east, when he was sure he was beyond the reach of Blaine and the others.

Frank had not moved a step when a gunshot echoed through the forest, and he dropped, scuttled to the tree line, and took cover behind one of the maples. The shot was not close, but the group could have split up. The others could have been closing in on him.

Seconds passed, and another gunshot rang out, slightly closer than the first one. Visibility was still limited, and given how poor the men from the village were at shooting, Frank suspected they had to be close to their target before they would risk a shot. They had to be close to even see a target, and there was only one other target in the woods.

Frank changed direction, returning to the east.

He needed to find Shane.

CHAPTER 24
HUNTING GROUNDS

Shane winced as he pulled a fingernail-sized chunk of bark from his cheek. The cold was numbing, but it made the pain feel different, and more biting. He breathed heavily, and his body was sore from the fall down the hillside. He only stopped long enough to dislodge the piece of wood and then took off at a run, dodging behind the tree trunks.

He was not sure who had taken the shot. To their credit, it was the best shot anyone had taken at him so far. The bullet had struck the tree right next to Shane's face, exploding the bark in a blossom that made him turn his face, but not fast enough to avoid shrapnel.

He'd intended to navigate around Blaine and the others, but there were three groups, not the two Shane had suspected. The third had stopped in the snow, apparently intent on waiting out the storm rather than doing their work. Their laziness had turned into an advantage when Shane stumbled upon them by accident.

There were three men, more than Shane cared to take on at the same time, especially when all three had rifles. He was less intimidated by them being armed than he would have been dealing with anyone who seemed remotely competent with a gun. But at close range, even one of the villagers would have been able to hit him if he was busy fighting two others.

Instead of challenging them, Shane turned and ran. The shot had been as close as anything they had tried, and he kept running for several dozen yards until he could no longer see them. He knew they could not see him through the snow when he stopped to pluck the wooden shrapnel from his face and get his bearings.

The second shot rang out nowhere near him, and he suspected somebody was just shooting at shadows. Nevertheless, he started running again, weaving through the trees.

He heard shouts behind him. The other groups had caught up with the one he had found. They knew what direction he was headed. They wouldn't give up too quickly, so he would make them work for it.

Shane headed west, away from where he wanted to be, hoping to find more difficult terrain that would make things harder for the others. If he found more ridges and ravines—slippery places that put his hunters at risk of injury—he would use them to his advantage.

The people on the island seemed more like hobbyists when it came to a self-sustained lifestyle. They had to be hard workers to survive the way they were, but Shane suspected a lot of that was the other people in the village, the older couples and people who had really committed to a natural lifestyle. People like Blaine were hangers-on, parasites who benefited from the work of others. At least, that was his impression.

That laziness made Blaine a poor choice to hunt someone and to be the muscle Mallory had chosen him to be. That was the reason he had fired a single-shot rifle and not thought to reload. That was the reason he would not be successful in hunting Shane.

Despite his disdain for the man, Shane did not underestimate him. Just because Blaine was not fully competent didn't mean he couldn't get off a lucky shot. Or, if his crew cornered Shane, that Blaine couldn't finish the job he'd come out there for.

There might have been some debate in the village, especially among those who were unaware of what kind of person Mallory was, but in the forest, that debate had been settled. These men sought to kill Shane and Frank, not talk to them. It would be a simple execution if they had the opportunity, and they would likely leave the bodies where they fell.

The storm raged, and the wind switched direction again, barreling down from the west, and hitting Shane full-on. The wind tore through the trees almost horizontally, blasting at him but doing the same to any who followed.

The forest ahead of him grew uneven. Little hills and valleys separated the trees, allowing some to grow higher than others and making the landscape harder to make out. Shane circled one of the hills and slid down a slight embankment into a snowy ravine, well-covered by trees that leaned toward it.

The edge of the ravine was concealed by a slight overhang, and he shuffled awkwardly along the length, leaving no tracks for the others to follow.

He reached the end of the ravine and found the smallest trickle of a stream, probably something attached to the one he had fallen into before. It cut a swath through the woods like a knife had been dragged through the dirt. There, he found a small hollow in the wet soil, enshrouded in roots like spider webs, away from the snow. He crept inside and pressed his back to the cold soil, hidden from view, and waited.

Shane took the time to catch his breath. The wind couldn't reach him hidden in the root den, and though it was not warm, it was a nice respite from the storm. He waited there, in the dark, and listened. Hiding his tracks had been impossible given the speed with which he escaped, but Shane anticipated being followed. He counted on it.

Once Blaine and the others reached the ravine and lost Shane's trail, they would separate. It was the most logical thing for them to do. At least one group would come toward him. Three men, and Shane was prepared for them. Those were odds he was comfortable with.

Ten minutes had passed when Shane heard feet crunching toward him through the snow. He stayed still, his back to the dirt wall and exposed roots hanging in his face, watching the ground in front of him. Someone grunted, and a man jumped down into the trickle of a stream.

"You got anything?" The man turned in a half-circle. From where

Shane hid, he only saw up to the man's knees. Anyone looking for him would have had to crouch and push past the roots into the impromptu den.

Someone else yelled a reply, but Shane couldn't make out the words. They sounded close, but not close enough.

Shane struck when the man turned. He pulled the man to the ground, taking out a knee and using his weight to yank the man down from the other side. He forced him face-first into the frozen, muddy bank. Whoever it was fell hard. Shane didn't concentrate on the man's face and didn't recognize the glimpse he caught, but he covered the man's mouth as he quickly slipped his arm around the man's neck and pinned him in place.

"How many of you?" He whispered into the man's ear.

The man called for help, but his cries were muffled by Shane's hand. Shane squeezed his neck harder until the man shut up and then tried again.

"You can answer or I can keep squeezing your neck. How many?"

He carefully pulled his hand from the man's mouth, giving him just enough room to answer. The man gasped, drooled, and made a mess of himself and Shane, and then yelled for help again before Shane clamped his hand back down and leaned his weight forward, putting more pressure on the man's neck.

The villager struggled, but it was short-lived. The pressure on his carotid artery was too great, and he quickly slipped into unconsciousness. Shane left him there in the mud, taking his rifle and hat and heading down the stream.

He found the other man a moment later, walking on the edge of the ravine. Shane had slipped the hat from the unconscious man onto his head and approached the second villager holding the rifle and waving.

"Any luck?" The new man shielded his eyes from the snow.

Shane's head was down, and he shook his head as he got closer.

"Some," he said when he was within range.

The butt of the rifle crunched into the villager's face, breaking his nose. He fell in a heap, bleeding profusely, and Shane bent to check on him. The man was not unconscious, but he was badly hurt. Another quick sleeper hold, and he went limp in moments. Shane unloaded the weapon, throwing the bullets into the snow and the gun in the opposite direction before leaving again.

Shane fired the rifle he'd taken from the first man, aiming at a nearby tree, and then ran down the bank of the stream to the west. The others would close in on the two unconscious men before they froze to death if they were lucky.

While they were distracted checking out the gunshot, Shane put as much distance as he could between himself and the villagers. The stream curved to the south, so he climbed the bank and entered the forest proper, continuing northwest.

He had only been running for a few minutes when a figure came at him from behind a tree. The bulky winter jacket meant it was not a ghost. Shane had nearly thrown a punch before he recognized Frank's face, not Blaine or one of his men.

Frank's fist was raised as well, and for a fraction of a second, both men were stunned.

"I thought they'd shot you," Frank said.

"Tried," Shane admitted. "Two of them are unconscious about fifty yards back there. The others will come to investigate."

"The woods are clearer to the north. We can double back east and get to the cave. They'll give up before long, and then at first light tomorrow, we can try for the boats again," Frank suggested.

It was as good a plan as any. They needed the buffer in time before they returned to the boats. The guards would expect them, and so would Mallory. But early in the morning, with a group of undisciplined, untrained guards, it would be much easier to get the drop on them and leave without being noticed.

As they made the shift to the north through the blowing snow, movement caught Shane's eye before they had traveled a handful of feet. A figure was crawling through the trees like an animal.

Shane had not seen a living thing on the island besides the villagers, and he did not believe the movement he saw was an animal. It was the ghost, mostly obscured by the storm but pacing them through the trees.

There was something different about it as Shane watched, nodding to Frank so the other man would be aware and on guard. It was hard to put his finger on what was wrong, but there was a different feeling in his gut. Something had changed.

Another shot rang out. Blaine stood next to a tree just far enough away that he was barely hidden by the snow, his face uncovered. He shouted words that Shane couldn't hear.

The ghost would have to wait. Shane and Frank started to run.

CHAPTER 25

TO THE EDGE OF THE EARTH

The wind raged. The storm was now stronger than ever. The violent power of the wind seemed almost personal as it beat down on Shane and Frank. Impossibly, it had shifted direction again, coming from the east once more. Shane no longer doubted that the storm was unnatural. The ghost was manipulating the weather or creating one of the most effective illusions that he had experienced.

Regardless of the reason, the storm was brutal, and the temperature continued to drop. Bundled against the elements as best as they could, Shane and Frank powered forward, trudging through the snow, and pushing back against the storm that urged them away from the eastern shore.

Blaine and his men could have been fewer than five yards behind and Shane would not have known. The swirling snow cocooned them, hiding almost everything. Even the trees remained hidden until they were far too close.

Soon enough, the sound of the world around them changed. Beneath the moaning of the gale-force winds through the subterranean caverns, there was a different roar. A constant susurration, loud and never-ending. They were approaching the ocean, and the waves were crashing against the island, loud and unyielding.

The eastern ledge came into view, a low-lying shadow that gave way to more gray beyond. Shane stared out at where he knew the ocean should be but saw nothing. The snow had concealed it, swallowed up the Atlantic, and left them nothing but a sheet of white and gray to look at.

"It's like the end of the world," Frank remarked.

"Not yet," Shane said.

He led them north along the ledge, looking for the path they had seen earlier in the day. The fury of the snow buried their tracks almost immediately. If the villagers were still following them, they would be hard-pressed to find which direction Shane and Frank had gone.

Progress was abysmally slow. Neither Shane nor Frank could find anything that looked familiar. Shane was certain it had to be north of where they came out of the woods. He didn't think they were anywhere near close enough, but the landscape was so unfamiliar in the storm.

They continued north, looking for any familiar territory or a path that let down until it became clear they must have overshot their goal.

"We have to go back," Frank said.

Shane nodded. The storm was as brutal as any he'd experienced. They needed to find shelter or they wouldn't make it through the night. They had to find the cave.

They retraced their steps with the unseen ocean on their left, raging in the diffuse white of the storm. Shane took the lead, and they passed what Shane recognized as the point where they started and then continued southward, still with no sign of the path to the cave.

"Think we've played this game long enough," a voice shouted over the wind.

Shane turned and saw Blaine, his rifle raised and pointed in Shane's face. He was so close that Shane was surprised he had not seen the man coming.

Blaine took a step forward, and a second man joined him. A third and a fourth appeared, and Shane and Frank were pushed closer to the edge with the ocean below. Snow and ice were caked in Blaine's spotty beard and eyebrows. He looked foolish, but he still grinned ominously as he kept Shane in his sights with an unmistakable look of smug satisfaction.

"It's loaded this time," Blaine said. He pulled the trigger.

Nothing happened. Blaine's eyes widened, and he tried again. Snow had clogged the hammer mechanism. It didn't even pull back when Blaine tried the trigger. The weapon was too old, too unreliable, and too frozen.

Shane pulled the gun from Blaine's hands and threw it aside, following through quickly with a punch to the man's face, reopening the wound of his broken nose and causing it to bleed again. The second man brought his gun to bear, and Shane barely had time to notice before the man screamed and was thrown over the edge of the island.

The ghost scrambled forth from the snow, looking over the edge as though surprised by his actions, and then bounded toward Frank, the next closest person.

Blaine was on the ground, grabbing at Shane's coat, and pulling him down. Frank dropped as the ghost lunged at him, and Shane lost track of what had happened as he planted an elbow in Blaine's face, targeting the same spot.

The wounded man squealed and put both hands up to his nose. Shane punched him again, forcing his hands into his face this time, and then brought his knee down onto the man's neck, looking to see how Frank was doing.

The ghost was gone, and Frank was on the ground, his hands up, gloves missing, and iron rings exposed.

"Get—"

One of the remaining villagers yelled something, but the words were lost as a fleshless hand reached around and tore out his throat. Blood sprayed through the snow, painting the ground red, and Shane left Blaine behind.

The fourth man was already running as Shane tackled the ghost. The spirit had sunk his teeth into the dying man's neck, biting and slurping at the bloody wound, but everything he pulled out fell to the ground beneath his grotesque form.

Shane pulled the spirit off the dead man and was struck suddenly by the fact that this was not the ghost that he had fought. Its face was chewed, the bottom jaw especially full of deep gouges, and it looked as though someone had eaten the left eye from the ghost's head. It was just as mutilated as the other spirit, but it was not the same one. The wounds were unmistakably different.

"Who the hell are you?" Shane pulled one of the ghost's arms around its back and subdued it.

Like the ghost he had previously fought, this one was energetic and surprisingly agile. But it was less intelligent and had less tact and strategy. When Shane pulled its arm, it reacted more like an animal than a man. It writhed and bucked, struggling to get free. Its movements worked against itself, giving Shane extra leverage, until the exposed joint in its half-eaten arm snapped at the elbow, and the appendage broke in two.

Blaine was back on his feet, staggering and dumbfounded. His men had abandoned him, save for the corpse lying in the snow, and all he could do was watch as Shane battled the spirit.

Even with one arm, the ghost struggled and fought, refusing to back down. Its one eye was cloudy and moved furtively. It wouldn't focus on Shane or anything else. It was hard to imagine how it saw anything.

Shane tried to keep control of the situation, to keep the ghost pinned and subdued as best he could, but its body was slick and greasy. Not wet like it had been coated with oil, but something thicker like lard. Even with gloves, it was hard to hold on to the ghost. The fact that it refused to stay still made it nearly impossible to control.

Losing an arm did not slow it down. The ghost reacted as though it had always been armless and there was no adjustment to be made.

Shane struggled to keep a grip on it, but the ghost moved in a quick, unexpected jerking motion. With a kick and a body roll, the ghost knocked back into the snow and was free.

A smarter foe, a living man, or the ghost that Shane fought previously would have capitalized on that moment. It would have pounced on Shane and killed him. But this ghost was chaotic and foolish. The moment it lifted its head, free from Shane's control, it set its eyes upon Blaine.

Blaine screamed as the ghost jumped on top of him. It leaned in, parting its jaws, and bit the man's nose. Blaine's scream rose an octave, and just as quickly as the attack began, it ended. The ghost vanished for the second time, forced back into the storm by one of Frank's iron rings. He had stood between Blaine and Shane, observing the fight but not wanting to get in Shane's way.

"It's gone," Frank said to calm Blaine down.

The villager panicked and struggled, pushing himself through the snow and escaping Frank as though he were the one attacking. Teeth marks on his broken nose showed how close he had come to losing it. If Frank had been a second slower, the ghost would have torn it off.

"Blaine!" Frank shouted, finally getting the man to shut up.

"It was… it…"

Whatever Blaine was trying to say, he could not vocalize. Shane was on his feet again, unconcerned with the man or his ramblings. He heard the snarl as the ghost came back out of the storm, returning from its haunted item.

Despite the satisfaction he probably would have received watching the ghost tear Blaine to pieces, Shane intervened, cutting off the ghost before it could attack the man again. He met it face to face, and it did not slow when it saw Shane. It ran with a loping gait, using its one good arm to steady itself, with the half appendage on the other side twisting and flopping about uselessly.

The ghost collided with Shane, and he took it to the ground for a second time. Frank pulled Blaine away, the other man too stunned to back off on his own.

"You're definitely not as smart as your friend." Shane wrestled with the spirit and kept its jaws away from his face. As the fight progressed, it became less like a man and more like a wild dog. But the lack of intellect worked to Shane's advantage, and getting the upper hand was easier the second time around.

The ghost snarled when Shane pinned it a second time after temporarily losing his grip. He pulled the spirit's remaining arm behind its back and held it there to get it to settle down. The ghost was in a frenzy. It didn't seem to care that it was putting itself at risk or that Shane had permanently wounded it.

"Have it your way," Shane growled.

Pressure was easier to apply now that he had better control of his target. He pulled the arm away at the shoulder, popping it loudly out of joint. The appendage fell loose and vanished as though it never was.

There was nothing to be learned from the spirit. Armless now and unable to defend itself, the ghost gnashed at Shane by twisting its head around and clamping its jaws shut in the falling snow. The spirit Shane had fought before thought and strategized like a man. This thing was no man.

Annoyed, Shane grabbed the ghost's head and twisted the skull, snapping its neck. He then slammed his elbow harshly into the side of the mutilated and half-eaten face, right next to its ear, and crushed the bone. It shattered and the ghost's body gave way, bursting, and then vanishing from existence. Shane was thrown several feet by the explosion.

Blaine looked horrified. Upon seeing the destruction of the ghost, whatever fight he had in him died with it. The man turned and ran, staggering through the snow as quickly as he could, following the fading footprints of his companion back toward the village.

Frank did nothing to stop him, though Shane couldn't blame him. He was tired of Blaine, and if the man hadn't left on his own, Shane would have done something more drastic. He had a feeling that Frank would not approve of the ideas he had for dealing with Blaine. First and foremost, Shane thought throwing him off the ledge into the ocean might be the best thing. The point was moot now.

Shane got to his feet and Frank came to his side as he dusted the snow from his coat.

"He was like an animal," Frank said.

Shane nodded.

"He was. And he wasn't our ghost."

"What do you mean?"

"Not the same ghost," Shane said. "The one I fought was smarter and faster. Different wound patterns. Different body types. They look similar. Whatever killed them was the same, but there is still another ghost on this island."

"Or more," Frank said. He wasn't wrong.

"And potentially whatever killed them in the first place," Shane added. If the ghosts were cannibals or trying to be, their killer could have been, too. And there was no reason to believe that it had been alive.

The storm still raged. Shane approached the dead man on the ground and stripped him of his gloves and coat. Frank frowned and Shane tossed him the jacket.

"We need it more than he does," he said.

"I suppose so," Frank conceded.

They continued along the eastern wall until they came across the path down the side of the cliff. It was precarious in the snow, buried deep, and battered by the wind. They risked death by descending, but it also meant that not even Blaine would follow them. If the original ghost showed up again, they would deal with that when it happened.

The cave was deeper than Shane had thought when he had seen Alina there. They headed in a distance and found a place out of the direct wind to build a fire. With the gear Alina had given them and the coat from the dead man, they could stay warm through the night. As for what happened after that, Shane would worry about it when it happened. The blizzard needed to break first. He needed to make a real plan about how to proceed. The islanders wanted them dead. There was at least one more ghost. And there was no way to know what the weather would throw at them.

With the boats on the far side of the island, they had set themselves up for a hard day ahead, but they were still alive. They were out of the blizzard. And they would survive the night.

That was all that mattered.

Epilogue

Blaine felt the sweat trickle down his spine. Just running through the snow was causing his legs to burn. The muscles strained and screamed with each step, but he couldn't slow down. He couldn't even bring himself to look back the way he had come.

He had never seen the island spirit up close. He had not imagined anything like that. It was a nightmare, a horror that had no business existing. When it had attacked him, it smelled of rank, rotten meat. Even with the swirling wind and the snow, it rolled hot over Blaine's face and made his stomach turn. It was all he could do not to vomit as it leaned in and parted its jaws.

The teeth that sunk into his nose were like ice. He thought for sure he was going to die. He thought the thing would chew off his face, crunch through bone all the way into his brain, and devour him there in the snow. He'd be a bloody, messy corpse, just like Donovan.

God, Donovan. The blood spray was like something from a movie. Blaine had never seen a man die like that. It was so fast. So easy. The monster didn't hesitate.

Blaine didn't know if any of the others were alive. He had set out from the village with eight others after they'd seen the dock flare. Three groups of three. They were ready to track down Benedict and Ryan, kill them on the spot, and be done with it. The blizzard would swallow them, or they could be tossed into the ocean. He didn't care. Neither did Mallory.

It was so hard to track them through the woods. Blaine had never tried that sort of thing. Back in the world, he spent most of his years working odd factory jobs. He'd last as long as he could until someone fired him for missing too many days. He had a bad habit of sleeping in or getting too high to remember to go to work. Then he'd move on and work somewhere else for a few more months until it happened again. He had never been a skilled man.

He resented the idea that he needed special skills to do a menial job. No one needed skills to work in a factory or a warehouse. He'd also resented the grind. Working another man's schedule. Be here at seven every morning or else. Clock in and clock out or else. Then pay the rent on time and keep the property clean. Pay taxes and insurance. Everyone pulled him in a dozen directions, and he wanted none of it.

What he wanted was to do what he wanted, when he wanted. He found that at Maple Grove. Or he thought he had. Mallory could be a hard ass, but all he had to do was haul crates of syrup to the island and sell them with two other people at the market a few times a year, and she didn't care what else he did.

It was a hell of a way to live. He got a cabin that was small but cozy, and he didn't have to pay for it. People cooked meals for him every day, and more than one of his new neighbors grew pot and were happy to share. Blaine was as happy as he'd ever been.

Learning about the spirit and the island had been a trip. He hadn't bought into it. Mallory had her flighty ideas about sacrifice and the cycle of giving and taking, life and death. Most times, he'd zoned out when she talked about it. She was an old-school hippie. Vegan, smug, and too self-important. A real pain in the ass. But he stayed on her good side because he knew where his bread was buttered.

And then this.

He didn't like Shane Ryan from the moment he saw him. He looked like a jarhead. And Benedict, for all his attempts to sound like everyone's buddy, was no better than a cop as far as Blaine was concerned. Asking questions and investigating what happened to Jackson. Jackson was an idiot, and whatever happened to him was what happened to all idiots.

The last thing Blaine wanted was to lose what he had on the island. Nothing was waiting for him on the mainland. He had no home and no job. He hadn't paid taxes in he didn't know how long, and if the government tracked him down again, they would have words. He wanted none of that. In his mind, there was only one way to get rid of troublemakers who brought attention to the island or what went on there. He had to make sure none of them left.

Most of the people on the island were too soft to make decisions like that. Blaine was not soft. He had what it took. He never killed anyone, but that didn't mean anything. He'd never needed to. He had guts, willpower, and determination. He was stronger than anyone he knew.

But then the storm, and those goddamn people. Benedict and Ryan, constantly picking at everything. Why couldn't they have just died in the cabin when they'd set it on fire? Why couldn't they have taken a hint and left after that first day? They grated on Blaine's nerves, especially Ryan. He was so smug and full of himself. Blaine could tell that Ryan thought he was the toughest guy in the room. Blaine hated him.

Blaine would have killed him. Everyone saw. He'd pulled the trigger. He would have done it. He'd just never used that gun and didn't know it only had one shot. Then Ryan had broken his nose. Goddamn Ryan.

Ryan had killed the ghost. It hadn't made sense, but it had happened. Blaine saw it. Ryan broke off its arms and then killed it. It was already dead, but Ryan killed it. He wasn't human.

That was why the gun hadn't worked in the blizzard. Ryan had done it somehow. He had some kind of powers or ability. He was a monster just like that thing. He'd probably brought them to the island. He'd probably killed Jackson. Shane Ryan was the real monster, and Blaine was going to kill him.

The cold burned his feet. He wanted to give in and drop to the ground. He wanted it all to be over, but he had to get to the village and get a better weapon. Ryan and Benedict would come soon, and he was the only one left who could stop them. This time, there would be no hesitation and no mistakes. This time, he'd blow Ryan's brains out of his skull.

The snow blasted on him, and it felt like ice picks being driven into his face. He was close to the village, though. He would be there soon. There was a gun in his cabin, one he'd taken years ago from another short-term resident who'd vanished, a sacrifice to the island. It was a revolver, and it was still loaded. Six shots. He'd show Ryan who was stupid. Blaine wouldn't miss with six shots. And that gun wasn't frozen.

He couldn't feel his feet by the time he reached the edge of the village. He fell down the small ridge, rolling through the snow until he came to a stop at the end of the road that led to the Great Hall. No one was out; everyone was smartly tucked away in their homes, probably huddled around their fire with blankets, enjoying the warmth.

Blaine trudged through the snow, breathing heavily and trying to keep his panic in check. He needed to focus. He returned to his cabin, pushed in the door along with a pile of snow, and stumbled to the chest he stored under his bed.

A fire was still burning, and it warmed him but not fast enough. His hands felt fat and clumsy as he struggled with the padlock to turn the dial. His fingers had no coordination or finesse. It took what felt like an impossibly long time to get the combination to work, and then he pulled the lock and opened the trunk.

The inside was a mess of random items. Some dirty magazines, his weed, a few bottles of alcohol, and the little bit of cash he had to his name. The gun was buried under it all, and he pulled it out. Six bullets would be more than enough to take out Ryan and Benedict, too.

He left the trunk open and stumbled back out into the cold, his hand shaking. All he could see was snow. It was the worst blizzard he could remember, and the island had had bad ones in years past. This was so much more.

On numb feet, Blaine made his way to the stone altar in the center of town. From there, he would be able to see Ryan and Benedict no matter which way they came from. Mallory didn't like people near it, but Mallory was tucked away safely in her little cabin, and she wouldn't need to know anything that happened until it was done.

Blaine paced around the stone to keep his feet warm. As long as he kept moving, he would be okay. The constant circling stamped down the snow and made walking easier. He had his own little path. It was easy to move and easy to see everything. They would show up soon enough, and when they did, Blaine would kill them. He would prove to everyone that he wasn't a joke.

It was hard to tell how many minutes passed. The cold kept taking hold of Blaine's thoughts. He was concentrating on what he was doing, watching every direction, and watching for Shane Ryan, but the cold was so intense. He hadn't realized someone had approached.

Blaine stopped, facing the path to the east. Between the cabins to the east was a shadow, the figure of a man standing there. Blaine raised his weapon and pointed it. He kept his arm steady. He wanted to look intimidating, but he couldn't prevent the shaking. The cold had sunk into his muscles so deeply that it was like his bones were frozen.

"Ryan!" Blaine's words were swallowed by the wind. "You're a dead man."

He pulled the trigger. It was harder than he wanted it to be. His fingers were numb, and they didn't want to respond. But it worked. The hammer cocked and slammed down. The recoil sent a painful vibration up his frozen arm. The sound was like an explosion, and he felt a thrill, a spike of excitement in his gut.

But Ryan didn't fall. Instead, he started forward, walking through the storm toward Blaine on unsteady legs. He walked like he was drunk, swaying and slow. Blaine fired again and again.

The figure drew closer, and Blaine saw that it was not Ryan. The man in front of him was nude and draped in scraps of gnarled flesh and torn muscle. It hung from his stomach like streamers. His chest was caved in, the bones pulled aside to reveal chewed and cut-up organs.

"No," Blaine whispered.

He unloaded the gun into the creature that stalked toward him. It did nothing.

"NO!"

He backed up, forgetting the path he had trampled for himself in the snow and fell over.

"It's not time," Blaine whimpered. "Mallory said it's not time. You took Jackson. You took Donovan and Gully! You don't need me. Please!"

The monster did not speak. It had no lips. There were gouges in its cheeks and chin and nose. It looked like someone had chewed them off. The biggest muscles of its arms and legs were gone, too. Its body oozed while it walked, and two clear, brown eyes stared into Blaine's.

"Please!"

He turned, scrambling away as the ghost paced toward him as though it had all the time in the world. Blaine's gun was empty, and he had no other weapon. He crawled through the snow on his hands and knees, trying to get to his feet and make his arms and legs work the way they were supposed to. He was so cold, and everything was so numb and unresponsive that he couldn't do it. He just crawled like a pathetic animal.

He scrambled past the first row of cabins and then turned, looking back at his pursuer, only it wasn't there. The howl of the wind and the blowing snow drowned out everything that he could see or hear. And then, something grabbed him by the head.

Blaine screamed, but no one heard the sound. The thing that dragged him moved fast, tugging him out of the village and back up to the snow.

Back up to the woods.

Check out these best-selling series from our talented authors:

GHOST STORIES

RON RIPLEY
BERKLEY STREET SERIES
MOVING IN SERIES
HAUNTED COLLECTION SERIES
DEATH HUNTER SERIES

IAN FORTEY
JIGSAW OF SOULS SERIES
CULT OF THE ENDLESS NIGHT SERIES

SUPERNATURAL SUSPENSE

A. I. NASSER
SLAUGHTER SERIES
SIN SERIES

DAVID LONGHORN
NIGHTMARE SERIES
ASYLUM SERIES

SARA CLANCY
THE BELL WITCH SERIES
BANSHEE SERIES

For a complete list of our new releases and best-selling horror books, visit ScareStreet.com or scan the QR code below!

www.ingramcontent.com/pod-product-compliance
Lightning Source LLC
Chambersburg PA
CBHW050346030726
47503CB00008B/2639